# Sombras

## SHORT STORIES

# K CUBAS

**MILTON & HUGO L.L.C.**
4407 Park Ave., Suite 5
Union City, NJ 07087, USA

**Website:** *www. miltonandhugo.com*
**Hotline:** *1- 888-778-0033*
**Email:** *info@miltonandhugo.com*

Ordering Information:
Quantity sales. Special discounts are granted to corporations, associations, and other organizations. For more information on these discounts, please reach out to the publisher using the contact information provided above.

| Library of Congress Control Number: | 2025901947 | |
|---|---|---|
| ISBN-13: | 979-8-89285-450-4 | [Paperback Edition] |
| | 979-8-89285-449-8 | [Digital Edition] |

Rev. date: 03/12/2025

# Dedication

I would like to dedicate this to my loving and always supportive Grandparents they are amazing. My grandpa who had so many vibrant stories thank you for your imagination. My Close Family & Friends thanks for your support. I hope everyone enjoys my stories.

# Contents

# Only One

# Prelude

His hammer hit my shield with such force that it sent me flying. I hit the ground hard, dropping my shield a few feet away from me.

'How many have fallen?' I thought to myself, of all those carriers full of us warriors for his army, how many had already perished? How many cries had I heard since we had arrived? Had we all heard them? Of course, we had because each of us were linked to each other to find and fight each other. This is why we knew when someone perished.

We'd been fighting for days. I knew we were both exhausted, but we continued to fight but for what? I no longer wanted to fight I wanted freedom, but such were these wars to choose the One, the Elite Soldier, to lead the rest of us to unknown parts of the universe for him to continue his quest for dominance. We were world conquerors; we were the power that helped him be who he was we gave him soldiers to use as his tools, just nothing but disposable tools for him.

My friends and I were trying to stop him, the one that had sent us here, the one that needed us, he was nothing; without us we knew this. Yes, he was of a stronger race then we had ever known but we believed he could be stopped. So, we fought for this to survive; to recruit others to join us; we needed to continue our quest and I needed to win this fight because Malik was one of the ones who believed in Him and believed we needed to serve Him at all costs for his pursuit of conquering and there was no way in changing his mind, I had tried.

"Sareafea, Malik's booming voice rang in my ears "You're dead," he laughed "You were always so smug, now look at you; you're so pathetic!" he yelled.

He had already damaged my armor and broken my pauldron; my shoulder was bleeding heavily. He wasn't looking any better; he was heavily damaged, and he was one of the stronger ones. I knew his strength as he was fully armored like me. Our strength came from our reaper's with their power we could be unstoppable the stronger our will the stronger we were together.

I looked up at him.

He had been fully armored like me, but I had been able to hurt him and destroy most of his armor he didn't have much left. I was stronger than him, I knew that, but these past few days had taken a lot out of me and him. I knew now he wasn't worth saving no not him; he needed to die.

I can't die here, I thought we couldn't die here. I must finish what we started, we must be free; I knew others from our group were recruiting many and the ones who stood in our way, we fought and killed. There was no other way. We had to keep fighting them; they didn't understand that this was for all of us to be free and to not be unthinking, unwilling soldiers that, in the end, would be a sacrificial piece for Him. Yes, this was for us all to find a way to be free.

"We can beat him, just focus. We are stronger, you and I; I will always be with you I am your weapon, your Reaper combined we can do so much, we will win." I heard Silas in my head and felt his strength pass through me.

"Give me strength, all we have. Let's go, Silas," I thought back.

Rain was falling hard on us as we continued to fight; the sky was dark and full of clouds and the lighting shone our way.

Another hard blow: he'd broken my helmet this time, and I went flying again, my shield and helmet disappearing. I had fallen hard, barely able to get up.

I landed so hard that I had to dig my sword into the ground to steady myself and keep from falling to the rocks below.

I heard more screams and more voices, they were clear and full of anger and pain, mourning their loss, and I knew their freedom was gone. More mindless soldiers for him to do as he pleased to use to conquer more worlds to enthrall more people. I hated it, I hated all of this. I just wanted to be free.

Malik laughed "Weak, you're weak. I thought you'd put up a better fight, but it looks like you have no fight left in you; your spirit has fallen, your reaper will be destroyed and you along with it," he laughed, holding his side at a fresh wound I had recently given him.

He turned his head suddenly, side to side, and then said, "What's that? You don't want to die? You want the wars to stop? You want your freedom?" He laughed, turned his head sideways again, smirked, and tapped his head.

His talent, dammit. I had managed to keep him out of my thoughts my mind up until now, I was weakening, dammit.

"Get up, get up now!" Silas said with urgency "We must fight we agreed remember? We must end this now."

I got up and just barely dodged Malik's hammer. I looked into his red eyes, his gray skin bloodied, his armor more than half gone just like mine and his muscular body all cut up and bleeding like mine. He had many open wounds and so did I.

I blocked his attacks and managed to dig my sword into his side. He fell to the ground, holding his bloodied side. He stumbled and fell back, barely standing, and more of his armor disappeared, he hardly had anything left on him now. He was almost done, and so was I. He had cut me with his sharp claws on my exposed side, and I noticed we were both now severely injured now.

"Lucky shot," he coughed, "but you'll die today, I'll make sure to finish you," he said.

As more screams came through, more dead, I hated hearing that I hated the fights I looked at Malik, and he didn't seem fazed by what we'd both heard.

We were at the edge of the cliff, now both struggling to keep going with the wounds we had inflicted on each other but still we continued to exchange blows.

"Silas, Silas, we can't lose; this isn't the end, my friend" I said out loud, "Let's end this."

Both of us were now bleeding heavily. I saw my chance. I called Silas, and a blade appeared in my hand, and I dug the blade deep into his chest, he grunted. He grabbed my head and lifted me off the ground.

I felt as if my head would explode; I could hear my bones breaking. This was the end, but I wasn't going alone; he was wounded as well.

I pushed my blade deeper into him, he groaned with pain but didn't let go. I twisted my blade into him he groaned more and seemed in pain. He still had me, not letting go but continued bleeding heavily. He groaned more as I pushed my blade deeper. He was on his knees now, still gripping my head as I kicked him hoping he would let go. He was strong, he then suddenly stood up and flung me to the rocks below. As I was falling, I saw him fall too, my blade still in him disappearing and what remained of his armor disappearing, and I saw him fall not moving.

Was he dead? I couldn't hear him, but I knew at least we'd both lost. I hit the rocks hard; my bones cracked; they were breaking. I was weak; a fall like this wouldn't have hurt me at my full strength but the fight had drained me. I closed my eyes; this was the end.

My last thoughts were that it was finally over, it's finally done, no more fights, Silas I managed to touch my pendant. Silas voice came through in my head very low and quickly vanishing "Wake up, wake up, I'm here, I'm here, we aren't….." I never heard the rest; that's when everything faded.

I felt as if I were floating away, I was finally done.

"I'm sorry, my friends. I couldn't go on," I thought.

I knew they would continue their quest to be free; I just wouldn't be there.

I heard a voice so distant…I didn't know who it was. I closed my eyes for what I thought would be my final time.

# Only One

I have walked this earth a million times, always alone. I don't know where I came from or who I truly am. I've never known why I'm here or what I have been looking for. There's always been something at the back of my mind, like a fog waiting to clear, and I'm hoping that one day that fog will lift, and all my memories will become clear, but so far not much has been revealed. I'm still lost, always looking for my past, to see if I have a history to tell me who I am, where I came from, and what I am and what I'm doing here.

I've watched the world fall and pick itself up. I've fought in many wars. I've seen men cut each other down, kill the innocent, and perform unspeakable cruelties I have never made an impact and have always been careful not to stand out to make sure I always blend in and to never leave a mark in history. Others do but not me; I've always been in the background.

When I woke, I was naked and alone. I didn't have anything on me but this pendant I wore which gave me hope that one day it would bring some answers I felt like it was part of me. I have never wanted to take it off and have never felt the need to. It always felt like a part of me like I was meant to have it.

I began noticing that I never aged; I've been the same since I woke and discovered I had strength that others would give anything to have; I don't get injured; my skin can't be cut; I don't sleep much as I don't need much sleep to have energy, but I pretend to sleep.

Most times I wonder what the hell I am, but I've never found another like me to tell me where I came from; I can move incredibly fast if I want and can leap incredible heights; sometimes I feel as if I can fly.

I know all the fighting techniques and the many languages of the world. I have made friends with a few people who I've trusted to know my secret. They call me an immortal; I have, over the years, kept in touch with the descendants of the ones who knew about me. I am grateful that, like their ancestors, they have kept my secret and continue to help me in ways only they can.

I am currently on my way to see one of these friends, who says they may have found some information that can help me seek some of my answers to who I am.

I sense someone watching me as I move. I have felt that throughout the centuries, but I have never been able to pinpoint who it is or what it is, but I feel it, then it suddenly disappears, and I don't sense anything.

I made my way to my friend Dr. Joseph Mero. He's a retired professor in his late sixties. His silver hair and glasses remind me of his father, and his deep brown jacket and light camel top matching his dark brown dress pants with black dress shoes make me smile, remembering when he was young and how curious he always was and how he'd follow me around whenever I visited his family, holding him as a baby and seeing how much he had changed and grown throughout the years. Seeing him have his own family.

We exchanged a hug, and no one paid us any attention as they probably thought I was his granddaughter. We are left alone to chat after ordering dinner, he tells me that there might be some caves in the jungles of Brazil that may hold some answers to what I am looking for. He also tells me that his expedition teams have been uncovering some similar drawings around the world in places that hadn't been explored yet or in unlikely places, perhaps overlooked by other teams or perhaps these locations are too dangerous for others to venture.

I'm glad that Dr. Mero is my friend and is still helping me as his ancestors did before him and that he was able to find information I was not. He informs me that his team may have an answer for me, or at least something to help me understand myself.

He showed me some pictures. He seems excited by what his team has found. He tells me that his team sent him those pictures yesterday. As I look through the pictures, one stands out. I stare at it, then suddenly I say, "Only One," touching the picture.

Dr. Mero looks shocked. He adjusts his glasses, his green eyes glistening and full of wonder. He asks if I know the symbols, as he has never seen them before, and they have never been recorded until now.

I look at the rest of the pictures and nod yes. I recognized them and for the first time, I felt happy and smile. I tell him what it says, "Only One can return to the light to lead the fight," but other than that, the symbols on the wall are broken and I couldn't read anything else.

The Dr. gets excited and informs me he can have a flight booked for me right away if I want to go and meet his team. He says I can pose as a fellow archeologist; he will advise the rest of the team I will be heading there to meet them. I agree to go as I am very much interested in what the site may hold.

He will book the flight for tomorrow morning, and he will inform me of the details later tonight. We bid farewell and I thank him again.

As I walk to my apartment, I feel like I am being watched. I stop and look around, but no one is there that I can see. My necklace feels heavier somehow; it's strange and doesn't look like it's changed but it does feel heavy.

As I approach my apartment, I see a shadow at my window. I'm at my door in a flash. I open the door, and nothing seems to be out of place. I'm scanning the room when a figure appears.

I do the normal thing and inform them. I'll call the police and say that there's nothing worth stealing so they had better leave right away, and no one needs to get hurt.

The person laughs it sounds gentle and sweet they say, "You've really forgotten, haven't you? I heard you were dead but then again, I would have felt it, and so would we all have, am I right? Well, the ones that are left anyway we would have felt you perish. Don't you sense us anymore? What happened to you? You just vanished after your last fight, and no one could sense you; occasionally, your presence would appear ever so faint and keep disappearing. We could never find you until now." A female's voice spoke.

"Who are you?" I say turning on the light.

"We will talk again; go on your expedition and learn something; we will keep the others at bay for now. After all, there can only be one and we all must fight but just as a warning, your presence is getting stronger, and you won't be able to maintain this life you've made for so long. Watch yourself," she says.

She had a slim figure and long black and purple hair down her back, her face was beautiful, like a porcelain doll. She was fair skinned, and her eyes were lilac, which I've never seen on a person before. She suddenly jumped from the open window.

"Wait!" I rush over and shout, "Who are you and what's your name?" but she was gone.

The smell of lilacs hung faint in the air. I leaped from my window and tried following her, but she had disappeared.

For the first time in my long life, I felt I wasn't alone; it wasn't just me; there were others and the fight she had mentioned what was that? I needed to know more.

As I lay in bed, my necklace felt heavy and warm, and it gave off a faint glow. I felt a great sense of loss; suddenly, I couldn't explain it, and it hurt so badly. I thought I heard voices cries so full of pain, anger, and whispers. I couldn't make them out. Could this be from the meeting with the stranger? I didn't know but I sensed it could be. I thought I heard a faint voice different from the others, but I couldn't make it out. I thought it was calling me, I heard "Seraf" then nothing I looked at my pendant it glowed a little then stopped. I lay there for a while wondering what that voice was.

I had gathered my papers for the morning flight to find out more about the symbols and if I could make out their meaning. I felt that this was what I had been looking for.

In the morning, I go to the airport and board my flight and I'm off to Brazil to see what I can uncover about my past; I wondered who wrote those symbols and what I would uncover. I kept sometimes feeling a deep loss, like a part of me was ripping away. It felt painful and the whispers and cries filled my head. I needed to know what it was and if it had anything to do with the stranger and what did she mean she would keep them at bay? But who or what? I thought.

As I disembarked the flight, I was met by one of the archeologists from Dr. Mero's team and was taken to the excavation site.

They told me what they had uncovered and showed me all the pictures of the site. They also said they had been told by Dr. Mero to provide me with full access to the site, as I may know what the symbols may mean.

I see he hadn't told them I was able to read the symbols, I thought, always protecting my secret like his ancestors before him I was grateful.

I thanked them, took out the tools I had been lent by the Doctor, and followed one of the archaeologists inside the cave where they were excavating. Dr. Leon, a tall, skinny man with brown shaggy hair and large glasses who looked in his mid-forties, was the lead archeologist. He said he would leave me alone as it was time; they went home for the day, and he asked if I would be okay and if I needed anyone to stay behind with me. I told him I would be fine and no need for anyone to stay. He then told me that if I found anything new to write in the journal, they kept, they would go over it the next day.

I thanked them for allowing me to stay, as Dr. Mero had informed them to allow me full access. I bid them goodnight as they began clearing the site. They left the lights on the site, and I stepped inside. I didn't need the lights, but I kept them there anyway.

It was like I had been here before I looked around. I noticed some writing on the pillars, so I ran my hand on them, and I was suddenly taken to a different time. The pillars were white with gold & silver markings on them, and I could see what was written.

"Only one can return to the true light, to lead the fight; all the unworthy shall perish and return to the lines; they will be cleansed and will rise again and shall fight in his honor; only one will return to the true light to lead." I read it out loud, but I still didn't know what it meant.

A flash appeared in my mind I saw a large group of being's, some looked regular like myself others slightly different they were not just people like me, but different. Some looked muscular with gray skin; others had wings with beautiful colorful feathers, some with transparent wings like that of fairies or butterflies; some floated in the air, and others looked green like toads so many different species in one room. They all wore pendants all shaped differently. All so different in this room, but why? "What is this? Was it because of the writing or this mysterious ruler?" I muttered to myself.

It came as a rush into my memory, but I couldn't make out their faces; they were very unclear, blurred. I didn't know them, but I felt connected to them; there were so many here more than a hundred at least.

My necklace felt so heavy suddenly and it brought me back from that memory. I looked down, and the necklace began to glow. The chain around it became longer and it broke suddenly. The chain wrapped itself around my wrist and hand making a glove, the pendant floating in the air and as I reached to touch it, it suddenly expanded and became a beautiful sword. I've never seen that type of sword before; it was golden with winged handles, the wings seemed to move gracefully. I was so surprised I didn't hear someone approach.

I turned around to see a tall muscular male dressed in a tight green muscle shirt and green loose cargo pants; his army boots tightly tied. His tanned skin glistened and his gold-hazel eyes stared at me. He looked like a model. He was standing at the cave entrance, holding a large battle axe resting on his shoulder.

"I knew you were still alive "He said and continued, "He should have finished you when he had the chance, just like I made sure he was done and perished into dust. The mistake was thinking you would perish but it's all good. I finished the job with Malik and now I can accomplish what he couldn't and be just one step closer," he smirked.

"You have kept yourself hidden; How did you do it?" he asked, "How did you hide yourself?"

"I don't know what you're talking about, and I don't know what's happening," I said with a quiver in my voice and the sword in hand that seemed to feel just right.

"I, I came here to find answers. I don't know anything else except that I can read the symbols. I can see them clearly now. Like a memory before the writing disappeared with age. Who are you?" I asked.

The guy smirked, then laughed "Are you serious? What kind of hello is this? What the hell happened to you?" he asked. "Do you not remember me at all!?" he said.

He touched his chest, and the breast plated armor disappeared. Then he touched his chest again and the axe disappeared, becoming a pendant like mine but different.

"Put your sword away; I'm not here to fight. I came because Nemi asked me to; she told me where you were; she's always been good at tracking people and other things like that," he said "Well, apparently not good enough considering we thought we'd lost you until recently," he shrugged.

He walked up to me, my sword still in my hand and I was now in a defensive stance.

He waved his hand to dismiss what I was doing.

"Relax Serafae, I won't hurt you, though I could but I won't After all, Nemi seems to want you alive and is wanting to have you join us again. She seems to want to stay here; it seems she isn't interested in the wars, but she isn't against fighting the others either," he shrugged.

"My name is Leana, I say, and "What are these wars you're talking about?" I asked.

"Who are you anyway, and why do I feel such sorrow and dread and why am I suddenly hearing voices and whispers? I hear screams and then they disappear. Can you explain that? Why can I read these symbols? "What am I, what are you, and what is your name is anyway" I asked.

"My name is Iskender, and I am a fallen," he answered.

""Your name is Serafae, one of the fallen but I guess you've discarded that name and now use Leana. But my how have you've changed and how have you discarded what you've always been and known? A shame, really; you were great but wow, that's impressive, isn't it?" He continued, "You must tell me how you did this; quite honestly, I liked Serafae more, by the way," he said, looking up and down at me with a huge grin on his face.

This made me blush and I didn't know what to say.

"We did have fun, didn't we?" He grins again, looking at me up and down once more. He then shrugs "Well, that was eons ago; oh well, it was fun while it lasted." He shrugged.

He continued, "Now as for the wars, well, they've been going on for eons as I said, and they won't stop until every one of us well perished from this plane anyway, but I don't really feel like fighting; you see, I have it pretty good here, and I like these humans; they are quite entertaining." He smirked.

"When someone shows up, I make them disappear and go about my day; I hardly hear them anymore; it just means less of us are here now. I'm strong, you know but since your presence, it's like I've become stronger and it's looking like more of us keep perishing faster and our numbers are diminishing. That's when the real war will begin" He looks at me curiously as he continues speaking.

"You can put your sword away and relax," he says, waving his hand again to dismiss me.

"I don't know how," I shyly say. "I have no clue how it came out; this is the first time it's happened." My cheeks felt a little flushed embarrassed.

He chuckled, then sighed, "Touch your hand to your heart and call back your reaper the sword he pointed. Call it back by name or just see it as a pendant again; it will disappear," he says, "until you need it again. You and it are one; it will protect you, fight by your side as hard as it can and arm you with what you need. You can become fully armored the stronger you are, and I know you are, but I'm guessing, of course, you had no idea. Oh, and yes, I am fully armored. He gives me a huge grin again. "I like you and probably the ones that are remaining have quite a few tricks and a bit of extra surprises, he winks at me.

"After all, how do you think Nemi and I have survived this long" he said, raising his eyebrows. He gestured to me to tap my heart.

I did as he said, and the sword became a pendant again. It felt strange, like when it was becoming a pendant, it said something to me, but I couldn't hear it clearly.

Now he said, "I'm sure you have more questions for me so I'll make it as brief as I can and you can, then you can swamp Nemi with all the rest of your questions, but first things first, let's start at the beginning."

He sat on a fallen pillar in the cave.

"As I said, my name is Iskender, and I am what you call a soldier. As humans say, we are in a war to see who is the best of the best and once we get to the end, there will only be one meaning: when there's only one winner, that one will be welcomed back to the stars, where the strongest will serve under his command to lead the troops. We are world conquerors, immortals on this earth and on others, I would assume, and nothing can hurt us in this planet it seems, but we can hurt each other, that I'm not sure why, so don't ask me that." He said this as he noticed I was about to ask something.

He continued "You see, there has always been a war or something rather, and there have always been soldiers and of course one to be welcomed into his army, his "Grand Elite" army. I guess that's the Light. "Every few eons, there is a war. Whenever there are soldiers needed, it's like what you would call a recruitment process testing us to see who is stronger, who is the best of the best. Anyway, I guess you can call us aliens, as humans would say but we are above all warriors, but we are also trapped and in thrall, to him and his race.

We are all greater than humans and most other species. We're stronger, faster, and smarter; we each have our own unique gifts; some have more than others; we are what humans would never understand, Nemi and a few others no longer wish to join the fights; we want our freedom, you see, and so we have formed an alliance of sorts. Once we are the only ones left and refuse to fight, he will have to listen, as this will pause his efforts" He needs soldiers, as he is diminished right now; he needs us so he will have to hear us, he will listen.

"The sorrow and dread, the anger you feel, is each life of a soldier dying. Their weapons our reapers they cry out before they vanish along with their masters, as once they lose, they will no longer have free will and they will lose communication with their master's us and they will be enthralled, forced to follow him, and used as mindless weapons. You see, each of our weapons is part of our souls; they are our fighting spirits, they are what keeps us alive and fighting and to continue being ourselves thinking for ourselves until well we can't anymore if we lose, our protectors our partners we are no longer whole. If your Spirit is strong, you'll be more armored, may possess unique skills depending on your spirit and this will give you a fighting chance for survival. "He paused looked at me and continued.

"You had all this and more, but you've forgotten. I hope that you start remembering, as we need you back in this war. You have always been one of the strongest you and your reaper.

Now the symbols are not of this earth; of course, they are from ours so you can read them just like we all can.

We each differ, as most come from different regions of the galaxy but still, we all fight for him.

I'm surprised you were able to not feel anything until now. It's so strange to me. I've never seen anyone separate our connection; you see..." he looked at me curiously.

"Who is this Him, which you keep referring to exactly?" I mean, you didn't really explain when I asked.

He pauses, suddenly and jolts out of his seat "Nemi, she's calling to me; something is wrong; she's in trouble," he says.

"Let's go NOW!" He shouts and jumps out of his seat. Hurry there's no time to waste. He runs off and I run after him to get to this Nemi person. I wonder if she is the one I saw.

We start running through the jungle, the passing trees a blur as we leave them behind, I've never found anyone like me until now. I wonder what else I will find out.

End of Part 1

# Out There

# Prelude

In 2036, nuclear wars and chemical wars were going on all around the world so many people had been infected by a 'cure' that was supposed to heal everyone; it was supposed to protect humanity from infections due to the wars that polluted the earth and water it was supposed to protect but instead it destroyed what remained.

Yet there were still some rallies on the streets from people that believed there was something that could help continued to shout, "The cure is out there! We need a cure! Stop the wars, heal the world" Shouts of the rally gathered in a downtown federal building, one of the only ones remaining as most had been burnt down by protestors. There were also many rallies around large pharmaceutical companies that were handing out these so called cures, these medications, and vaccines to supposedly help people change their bodies adjust to toxins in the environment, and the rallies around hospitals that were packed with people trying to get in to the hospitals to get these cures and the hospitals that no longer had any room people were desperate and pushed on, not enough doctors.

The police that remained were everywhere, trying to keep the crowds at bay. They were armed and masked as no one knew exactly how this pandemic was being transferred from person to person. They figured maybe airborne; the police were ready to put down people who stepped out of line to try to keep the peace.

People continued demanding a cure for the wars that were going on and a stop to the wars. In the world, millions had already died, the numbers were staggering if they hadn't died. They had been infected and driven mad with this new virus strain that turned them mad, violent, bloodthirsty killers with no conscious awareness but still left them alert enough to fight back and form groups. These people needed a cure to get back their humanity but unfortunately none was available.

With no cure in sight, many scientists from all over the world were working together overtime to find anything to help with what was now a full-blown pandemic like nothing seen before.

They knew this was due to the original wars and original cures they had provided not being fully tested long enough to see what would happen over time and they had provided this cure at a rapid pace all over the world to slow down infection of the many diseases being spread.

Now people the ones that had taken this cure kept getting sick and they became something else what was supposed to be a cure was something no one could have predicted the world continued their wars but now a new was starting with the infected, so the wars raged on.

These pharmaceutical companies wanted to give people immunity and a chance to survive but it didn't work the way they expected, and the wars got worse, the air became toxic and the more cures that were made to help, the more they seemed to fail. It also didn't help that illegal labs all around the world were making their own versions and selling them to the desperate. This only seemed to mutate into diseases without cures, and it became dangerous to be outside so the people not exposed began to hide away.

The doctors and scientists continued to try to heal what was broken. They tested and tried to see if a cure could be made from a child grown in a lab that had not been exposed to the world as it was now, but this was never known to be true as most of the scientists died testing out their theories with nothing to show for their work so no one knew if they had succeeded.

Many more years passed, and many more people became infected not by only the cures but as well as by crazed people; even most of the scientists that had been working on a cure got infected. Their work passed on to those who weren't yet infected. The ones still trying to find cures went hiding and continued their work to bring back humanity in undisclosed locations.

They hadn't found a cure to bring back the people that had become violent and crazed. They hadn't been able to bring back the world, but the ones that were still alive continued to search, never giving up.

The world as I have been told ended in Madness and Chaos cities fell burned to the ground and the desperation ruled, people killed each other to get food and necessities it was chaos and because there were no longer governments, only Marshall Law ruled. Cities that survived built their walls closed themselves off and became self-sufficient and the world disappeared and talk of hope for a cure seemed to disappear along with any searches. People just seemed to forget to lose communication with each other but still, some people hoped that one day they could walk the free world again.

The cure was left to the few scientists that remained hidden and continued testing and hoping that one day they could see the world as it once had been.

# Out There

The woods stretched out for miles; all I knew was that I couldn't go out there alone. It had been like that since I was a child.

We trained in survival skills in the morning, then took breaks and continued to train every day. My father said I needed to learn to protect myself and survive.

I knew the monsters were out there, ready to haunt, and growing smarter each time. This was why I just couldn't leave the cabin alone; my dad had warned me several times not to wander out without his knowledge.

Sometimes at night I would hear laughter, screams, and howls. I didn't know where they were, but the sounds kept getting closer.

At the break of dawn, I watched my dad get the shotgun ready, the smell of gun powder filling the small cabin.

He started packing his bag with a sharp, long machete, some fishing gear, a trap, his gun, and his spear, which was made from light wood and easy to carry and handle but tough enough not to break. I looked at him; he looked so tired lately.

He always reminded me that the gun was a last resort since it would attract attention when it went off. He mainly said this to himself since I wasn't allowed outdoors when he was gone. He continued telling me that if things got bad and I heard the gunfire, I'd know it was no longer safe and I needed to leave without him.

I looked over at the spears leaning by the door; they were the ones he used to train me when there was enough light out, as he said that I should always know how to fight and to be able to defend myself if anything should happen to him or if we were ever separated.

I nodded at him, letting him know I understood.

Lately, the days seemed shorter, and we would probably be leaving soon as it was no longer safe since the laughter and howls seemed to be coming closer each day.

My father, before leaving, reminded me to make sure to bolt the doors and set the traps, and under no circumstance was I to open the door until he came back and provided our secret password.

Once he was back, he would go to the small washroom in the cabin and get cleaned up, and we would talk after. He would always try to bring me a small trinket for his trips, which I always looked forward to that.

He would train me daily and homeschool in subjects like science and labs and go over what I needed to do in case we were ever separated like he always did it was in grained into me to know what to do. He always said I would need to know these things to know how to survive without him, he always reminded me of this. He taught me about edible plants and how to cook them and find them and what to look for to make sure they were edible and what building to look for if I needed supplies or food if I couldn't find anything.

My dad looked at me and asked me to repeat his instructions as always. I said, "Set the traps, bolt the doors, don't open for anyone unless it's you and even then, you'll give me the password to let me know you're okay."

"Good" he nodded, told me he loved me, gave me a quick hug and set out on his way.

He also reminded me that if he wasn't back before nightfall, I would need to make sure I was ready to move when daylight came, as the creatures were sensitive to light so the best time to move was in the daylight. My dad also reminded me that these creatures remembered places and specific locations. He reminded me I needed to be cautious not to make too much noise or I would attract the attention of things out there.

He reminded me that I should always pack light and have just what I thought I would need and to start getting ready to move quickly. He told me where the next safe spot was and where I could look for food.

He made sure I knew the quickest way to reach the locations that would keep me safe.

I always had my bag ready, so I just nodded, and he went to catch some food, and I locked the door.

I stayed inside as the hours passed... I was reading old books my dad had about science, genetics, equations and formulas that I had to recreate and make as he had taught me. He always said he was proud of me and how far I had come. I checked my watch, and wondered, "Why hadn't he returned yet" .... Then I heard loud laughter getting nearer which scared me and then a voice saying something familiar. I wasn't sure what it said or if it was anything at all, I stayed still then I moved slowly to the door to listen.

Then suddenly a knock made me jump and then I heard the code. I quickly opened the door as fast as I could. My dad was there, and I let him in. He didn't do his usual routine and he seemed more tired, and I wasn't sure if he was hurt. I looked at him, he seemed a bit out of breath and panicked. He then took a deep breath and began his routine. It somehow calmed me to watch him do it.

He said, out of breath "I think they're gone, and I don't think I was followed, but we have to leave; it isn't safe anymore."

We stayed the night quiet as always, making sure we had everything ready for our trip in the morning.

At the break of dawn, I ate some rations and noticed dad was still sleeping. "That's weird," I thought he's always up before me.

I shook him awake and told him I was ready, and he needed to eat. He said he would be fine and grabbed my bag so we could leave.

I looked back at the cabin as we walked away. My whole life had been there. I was excited to finally leave but I knew we had to be careful; we had to move quickly and quietly. I knew the risks.

I tied my brown hair in back as my dad reminded me how these creatures, who once had been humans, were dangerous and killed just at the slightest sounds or movements. They seemed to be evolving and getting smarter, learning to communicate with each other to hunt in groups my father had warned me that even though they resembled humans they were totally inhuman things.

On the move, we searched some abandoned buildings that my dad said had been stores and contained food and necessities if we were lucky and he said they could be used as shelters. He said they had been abandoned, if not ransacked, during the wars. We looked for food and took a small rest.

We walked among the empty streets in what used to be a city and my dad told me as we walked the stories about the past and how it had been.

I looked around at all the buildings, the plants overgrown, and the earth breaking through the ground, cracking the pavement and grass growing through. All the stores were all boarded up. My dad said we should rest inside. He seemed tired and kept coughing very quietly. I thought I heard a chuckle but still, he walked with me. I sensed something was wrong, but I never asked, I was afraid to ask.

I heard noises in the distance; then it seemed to be growing closer.

I saw my dad smile and he told me he loved me. He then asked me to tell him what I had learned, and we went over everything about what I had learned as we walked, what I needed to do to create a cure and that I needed to continue to practice getting better to survive. He seemed upset, and suddenly I asked what was upsetting him, but he said that it was nothing.

We continued walking through the ghost town, and he continued with the stories of the past and how amazing it once was. It sounded great, I wish I could have seen it.

I noticed more plants wrapping around the light posts as we passed; it all seemed so beautiful and the broken glass on the ground was shining in the sunlight like jewels.

The abandoned vehicles on what used to be roads were dusty and empty, some were brooken.

I picked up a worn-out magazine thick with dirt and a book with yellow, worn pages.

My dad had told me about the wars and how the world destroyed itself and all the people, how they panicked, looted, and raged on the streets, causing cities to burn down, and how the government was nonexistent and how it had fallen and failed.

How these things that had once been human but now were in a sort of death state, still moving but their minds were no longer there. They had no sense of right and wrong; they were simply lost, crazed and oh so dangerous.

Over time, my father told me about how people had created walled cities that were made for people with no signs of infections, they built these places to be safe to help people find a refuge and to try to stay safe and to hopefully grow in population.

They then classified the infected into classes the ones that still seemed alive but not dangerous or not that anyone had tried to find out, but they seemed to be able to understand for a little while, but they would turn eventually. The rest they classified as mindless, predatory creatures; the slow-moving ones they had noticed weren't too dangerous and people could escape them if they were on their own, they had noticed they usually dried out and died as they would stop moving and remain frozen in place they walked in small groups or alone in larger groups they could be lethal.

The ones that seemed to still have kept most of their mind and thinking capabilities were extremely dangerous; they were the fast ones they howled and laughed maniacally they hunted and seemed to want to kill anything on site; there was no reason for it; they were just extremely violent and gruesome.

My father had warned me to stay away and if I ever saw one to be as quiet as possible, find a hiding place and wait for them to pass or wait to travel in the morning. The light was our friend.

He told me about the ones that had starved to death, the ones that were slower, and that most had died off as he knew but still to be careful.

He said what started out as a cure quickly turned into an infection crisis, then a global pandemic. The governments that were still around blamed each other and started attacking each other instead of trying to fix the problem.

They began chemical wars to stop the infected and the use of these chemical weapons wiped out nations and caused large damage to the earth. The waters became poisoned, and most animals began to die or mutate because of these wars the food sources were cut down dramatically.

As we were talking, I noticed my dad lagging, not keeping up, and short of breath. He suddenly stopped. I went to him and touched his face; it felt ice cold. I went into my bag, pulled out some water, and went to him again, but he pushed me back, told me not to come any closer. He took his bag off, tossed it beside me and told me everything I needed was in the bag to carry it with me as it was mine now. He said I knew what it contained, that I had been training for this and that I knew where to go. I nodded, He had told me there were other doctors in hiding and that I needed to find them. He told me never to stop. I was the hope what we needed, this bag contained all the research, and its contents were now mine.

He then told me to stay away from him and that he loved me, and this was what I was meant to do what I had been trained to do. He asked me to please make sure I reached the location he had shown me on the map.

I picked up the bag and looked up. I saw my dad begin to retreat away from me; his eyes were no longer hazel but black and his movements were no longer controlled but involuntary.

I picked up the bag and spear that had fallen where my dad had once carried them. I hadn't known he was infected; I never knew how it happened or when it had happened.

Through glassy eyes, I said goodbye to the man who had raised me and loved me all these years, to the man who showed me how to survive without him and what I needed to do to survive on my own to create an effective cure.

I looked up and realized I needed to move, there were only a few more hours of daylight left, and I needed to find shelter.

Dad would have wanted me to be safe; he had taught me everything I knew, including where to go to continue my journey, how to live, and to hopefully bring other survivors together to fix what the past had broken and to begin rebuilding the world. Dad said I was the key to fixing what was lost; he had taught me what I needed to stay alive and be safe. I knew I would make him proud, and I would do anything in my power to help this disease with all my father's knowledge.

"I promise I will survive; I will bring humanity back; I love you," I cried as I took the shotgun and shot him. I knew this would bring the hordes, but I knew he wouldn't have wanted to be that way to live without his humanity. My hands shaking, I looked back at what had once been my father and began to move towards the coordinates where he had said we or no I would find someone to carry out his work for the cure to save humanity.

## End of Part 1

# The Mine

# The Mine

It was almost summer break; everyone was already making plans; only one more week was left of school; and then senior year was about to start once we got back.

"What a bummer, everything's ending totally sucks," Annie said. "I'm going to miss this place because everything is going to change next year, you know we can't slack off anymore with college just around the corner." She said, fiddling with her curly brown honey locks, her loose shirt sliding off one shoulder, showing her black bra.

"On the plus side, lots of things change during the summer, and when we're back, we get to see everyone again and how they've changed or mutated. I wish there would be some new faces, but no one ever transfers in the last year that's for sure" Chris laughed, making a face, "You're such a child," Cloe said shoving him playfully. "But your right things get boring around here, that's for sure and after grad, we will be able to go wherever we want." she sighed and shrugged her shoulders.

"Final year, I for one am excited to get the fuck out of here, to finish my auto shop classes and graduate, get a free pass to a good school far from here and not be stuck working at the shop again. Yes, been good but I want more…. Just more, you know?" Chris sighed.

"So, M, anything exciting you're looking forward to?" he asked, opening his locker, putting his books away and taking out his coveralls for his shop class.

"Well, let's see summer at Nates for sure, getting drunk and having a blast with all of you crazies but other than that same old boring shit. Honestly, I rather be anywhere but back at this dump. I mean seriously, in this place for another year, I dunno if I can take it" I laughed.

Nate chimed in, "I for one, am looking forward to summer bikinis', tourist girls' hookups, and parties." Nate smirked, he looked at all of us, and we rolled our eyes.

"Umm Nate I think you're drooling a bit there." Cloe pointed to his lips. "As per usual, you're so typical," she said.

"Okay guys, gotta go check in. catch you all later." Annie said as she walked away with Cloe. They were whispering and laughing looking at Chris and Nate. They waved at us, arm in arm, together.

"I'm off too, later!" Chris said, heading towards the shop wing.

"Catch you later Nate and Chris!" I said, heading towards first period.

"Later M," they said as they headed to their classes. I walked away to first period all the time thinking of how much fun we would have in our last summer as seniors together before we all went our separate ways after graduation.

We had all grown up together and had been close since grade school. We never kept any secrets from each other; it had been one of our promises to each other to tell it how it was, even if it hurt or if it made some of us uncomfortable, but it had always been that way. We had all pulled each other through some hard times, cried together, laughed together, and were just best friends.

I had, however, noticed some things changing recently. We still hung out all the time; we practically lived at each other's houses. It was a small town; not much ever happened here without someone noticing. Lately, though Cloe seemed to be very distant, she kept saying she wished she could wake up somewhere different, like a different town or place. She really wanted to just leave this town. Her dad was a drunk and she slept mainly at my place or at one of the others. He had a bad temper when he was drunk and took it out on her, so she always said it was a bit much for her.

She wanted to leave and get out of this town. She said once we graduated, she was going to the city. She had saved up enough money to rent a place. She had invited one of us to go with her but that was up in the air at this time, though Nate seemed interested.

Finally, summer break came, and we got ready to head to Nate's parents' cabin. I couldn't wait. I loved it there. The fresh air by the lake was nice and secluded. We could do whatever we wanted, plus we had all grown up there. His parents were both doctors and they were hardly ever around, so it was like our get away. The fridge was always stocked and there was an open liquor cabinet available. They obviously knew we used it, but they were fine with that. Nate said his parents were the type to have him be somewhere they knew he was safe rather than be out somewhere he could get in trouble. We were teenagers, so they said it's better to have a place to go than be on the street doing something you'll regret later. I thought they were so cool.

"Okay, okay, so where the fuck are Chris & Annie?" I said, waiting in the parking lot with the rest of the group.

I'm sure I wasn't the only one who noticed them spending more time together, being all flirty and the "secret brushes" they had. Yup, hooking up, I thought but why not just say something?

I looked over at Nate because I knew something had gone down with Annie and him last summer; she had told me of course.

For as long as I can remember, it had always been the five of us sticking together since grade school. Annie, Chris, Nate, and later Cloe joined our group, and yes, we mostly had different interests, but that's what made it fun and why we were best friends.

When Annie and Chris rounded the corner, he had his arm around her shoulder. We all hooted and laughed. I looked over at Nate, he seemed a bit uneasy but gave a smile.

Her curly hair bouncing, a mid-drift shirt outlining her ample breast and her booty shorts outlining her figure.

"Okay, let's get this show on the road, guys. Now that we are all here, let's pile in and get the fuck out of here." Nate said he got in his car, with Chris going with him and we all followed behind them.

We arrived at the cabin, it was like a mini mansion in the woods, walking distance from the private lake. There was room for all of us; we each got our own rooms. This place was great; I loved it.

Annie and I went to change into our swimsuits and began dinner prep. We could hear Nate grilling Chris about Annie.

Cloe said, "So yes, Annie, what is up with Chris?" she asked.

Annie smiled and blushed, shrugged her shoulders, and gave a giggle. "I don't know he's just dreamy, you know; it just happened. I mean look at him, he has this sexy body with six packs and muscles and cute strawberry blond hair and green dreamy eyes and omg, he's so fun." she winked.

We all laughed; guess he was the flavor of the month.

We had a nice barbeque outside in the fresh summer air and drinks. I took a dip in the hot tub with Nate, Cloe, Annie, & Chris who were all over each other making out.

"Ok Yuck" Cloe said, "I don't feel like watching a live Porno" Anyone want to join me inside for drinks and movies?"

We started getting out of the hot tub following Cloe as Chris smirked and said, "Hey, maybe we can all have some fun together, ladies? Nate?"

"No thanks" Nate said, "Oh and I don't need any little swimmers in the hot tub and no one getting pregnant or whatever while we're out here, Shit!" He chuckled unenthusiastically.

I looked over at him; he was looking down at the ground as he had said that, clearly uncomfortable with the situation.

We all laughed as we left the new couple in the hot tub and headed in for some much-needed drinks and a movie binge.

The third day at the cabin felt oddly strange; it was too quiet and the usual laughs and giggles and just nonsense weren't there. It felt so weird.

At breakfast, we were divided, with Annie and Chris on one side and us on the other. I had to say something to break the silence because it was unbearable "Okay, people, just a few more days till we head back, let's plan some fun shit to do so I was thinking swimming at the lake maybe skinny dipping? Doing a big bonfire in the pit, talking shit about people getting pissed drunk?" I spoke.

That seemed to lighten the mood I got a few laughs. "M, you're great at setting the mood." Nate said, "Yeah, I'm down. What about the couple here, which is a mood killer, always disappearing on everyone." He spoke.

"Fine." they both said and giggled.

"Great, then we will do music drinks and laughs and just a fuck load of shenanigans for tonight, then it's settled. Let's have some fucking fun after all; we are only here for 5 more days, people!" Nate said.

We all cheered. Summer was looking great again, as it should.

"I'll tell Cloe once she's back," I said and started preparing some food for the party later.

Nate, Chris, and Annie went off to play video games, the guys laughing as they headed into the games room.

"That's a great sign." I thought they were getting back to normal.

Cloe suddenly burst through the doors from her morning run, her cheeks flushed and her blond hair in a tight ponytail. She matched her outfit down to her pink shoes.

She started talking quickly a bit out of breath "I went for a jog and did you guys know there's an abandoned mine near here!? It's patched up but it's there and looks so cool." "Where's Nate? "She said.

"He's in the game room with Chris and Annie," I said.

We went to the game room, and she told Nate what she had found. He said he knew it was an old, abandoned diamond mine that had been there forever, plus he added, "There's a scary story my parents told me a long time ago but I'm sure it was for scares," he said.

He told us that apparently the mine was closed because a lot of the miners kept disappearing and the ones that didn't were never the same; it's like they had been scared straight. "Apparently, a young guy and his girlfriend went there once, and they never came back out. Though I think they just ran away together," he said. "Also, apparently, you can hear voices calling for help but then no one is there. Cops have gone to investigate but they don't go very deep into the mine. I think they are too scared to go in and they just tell everyone to stay away from there. You must have run far to get there," Nate raised his eyebrows.

Cloe looked at me and Nate and said, "So, wanna go check it out? Who's up for a trip?"

"Well, there's nothing much to do around here," Nate said. "And I could use some fresh air and get away from all the lovey dovey shit, so I'm up for it. How about you, M?" he spoke.

"Why the hell not," I said, "let's pack some stuff before we head out though, okay?" I spoke.

Cloe jumped excitedly and gave me a hug.

We had fun that night with lots of laughs and jokes, just like always, it was great. At early morning the next day, we made sure we were packed up and ready to go.

We had some flashlights, glow sticks, and a few snacks because Nate said we'd need some. We packed a first aid kit, a fully charged satellite phone, some beers, and I was just about to close my bag when Nate said to hold on, he packed some condoms!? "WTF", I said, "seriously Nate, what is going through your devious mind?" I laughed.

"What! In a dark and secluded place, one of you is bound to get scared." He raised his eyebrows and continued, "You're welcome both to run into my arms. I'll protect you from all the spookies or maybe you might want to get warm, so body heat is the best. Since it's probably so cold in there, so make sure you bring a small blanket." A sly smirk crossed his face.

I cleared my throat and pretended to be his mom, "Nirvaan Char, you know you are to respect all women and do no funny business while you are under this roof or any roof," I sternly said. "So then, ummm, hell no!" I said with a laugh.

"Seriously M, full name, so not cool" he said, running his hand thru his thick black hair and making a pouty face his honey brown eyes looking up at me, he then smiled and stuck his tongue out.

Cloe also laughed but said, "You know, you could just ask." She winked.

Nate smirked, "Really, I didn't know I could, I'll keep that in mind, or we can just have some fun in the mine. Oh, and M, you're always welcome. I don't mind having two lovely ladies lay with Me." he smiled.

"Holy shit, I'm stuck with a bunch of horny people." I rolled my eyes.

"Chris, A," Cloe Yelled "We're about to leave, so get your asses out here." she yelled.

They both appeared out of breath Annie's bra strap hanging off her shoulders from the game room.

"Okay," Nate said, "We're leaving now so a few house rules." he cleared his throat.

"Don't break my shit, don't fuck everywhere, clean up after yourselves and make sure the satellite Phone is always with you. We have our phone, so you had better keep this one on. So please keep your fucking phone on hand. "Oh, please have some dinner ready when we get back; I'm sure we will be very hungry from this activity." He looked over at me and Cloe, who blushed.

36

"Yes, Sir." They saluted and laughed.

"This should be fun," Chris said.

We headed to the door "Later, guys, be good." I waved.

We left the cabin and got to the mine almost an hour later. Cloe was so excited she kept saying there was something shiny; she could see it, but it disappeared suddenly. She Yelped, "There's probably some diamonds in there!"

"Doubt it, this mine hasn't been active in ages, plus if there was, they'd be deep in the mine so whatever you saw definitely wasn't there," Nate said.

She hurried her flashlight, guiding the way, and Nate was right behind her; I began placing glow sticks behind us to help us find our way back to the exit and followed them into the mine. It started getting colder and damper the deeper we went in.

Cloe, excitedly said, "We should go deeper." she kept saying she saw something sparkling on the walls. She got so excited that she gave Nate a huge kiss and me a hug and a kiss on my cheek as she jumped up and down. "Let's go deeper," she said.

"I can go as deep as you want me, baby," Nate said.

"Auggh, Barf" I said and rolled my eyes.

This got a laugh from Cloe, she looked back at us and kept going.

As we went deeper, I felt as if we were being watched, I heard scratches on the walls. "Probably bats," Nate said when I told him.

Cloe took the lead, shining her light on the walls, saying they sparkled, and we hit the mother load.

She started picking at the wall, and when nothing came out of that, she said, "Awe boo, no diamonds. What a bummer, okay well, it's cold as fuck, so let's start heading back." she said giving a sad pout.

"I'll turn your frown upside down, Hun," Nate said.

"Well, guess so much for that spooky story; it looks like nothing is here," Nate said. "Yup, a real disappointment like everything else, Memo to self; don't expect much," he said.

We began to head back but I couldn't see the glow sticks were gone "What the hell!" I spoke, "I put them to light our way back I was making sure they were there!"

Nate said, "It's fine, we still have the flashlights, let's just go. I'm getting hungry; besides, I doubt we are that deep."

We let the flashlights guide our way, staying close to each other when the flashlights started to flicker, which was weird because they all had fresh batteries.

Suddenly, we were in the dark, in a damn cold cave.

We heard gurgling noises and scratching noises; the movements sounded fast.

"Everyone Hold Hands, Something Coming Our Way, Let's Go!" I yelled.

We all started running towards a faint light right ahead; assuming it must be the exit.

Suddenly Cloe screamed, she yelled that something was on her, "Nate!" I yelled, "Get the phone! The Phone, Nate!!" He quickly went into my bag and got the phone out. Cloe was screaming "Help" the whole time. While I was trying to find her in the dark.

We got the phone out and it lit up. He pointed to the light around us. What we saw were creatures with gray skin, shining black eyes, and sharp teeth. They retreated as Nate pointed the light toward them.

"Cloe!!" I yelled; "she had just been here. Where was she!? Cloe!!" I yelled again.

We could hear Cloe's distant screams, how had she gotten so far from us? Nate started freaking out, he just said, "Shit, this is bad. Fuck, we must get out of here but fuck, we can't leave her, we can't leave her." He said in a panicked voice. I found a glow stick at the bottom of the bag and broke it, lighting our surroundings.

"How did she get so far away from us, she was just here, she was…?" Nate was mumbling to himself.

The creatures retreated quickly, and I grabbed Nate's' hand and started running towards the light pulling him with me.

The whole time he kept saying, "We can't leave her, we can't leave her," as I yanked him forward.

As we were running, the phone rang, making us both jump. Nate answered it, his voice shaking. We heard Chris's voice, "Where the fuck are you guys?" And in the background, Annie yelling "Dinners ready."

"Hey, what's happening hello?" Chris said, alert sounding in his voice.

"Help us!" Nate yelled. "Help! She's gone, she's gone! We are in the mine, call the cops or anything, please help Cloe. Oh god, Cloe, she's gone, please help!" Nate yelled as we continued running towards the exit.

Annie came on the line, "What happened? What's going on? Is Cloe, okay? Are you trying to scare us? It's so not funny you know."

"Call the cops!" We both yelled as we ran towards the light.

Something scratched my arm, and I screamed "M!" Nate grabbed me and we continued running towards the light. When we finally reached the outside, the sun blinded us and looking back, I saw nothing. All I could think of was Cloe and I just burst into tears and fell sobbing on the ground.

We were both bleeding and crying, holding each other.

The police came with Chris and Annie; they ran towards us and held us.

"What happened?" Annie asked. "Where is Cloe? "She sobbed as she saw me crying, she held me, as I broke down.

Nate kept repeating, "Cloe, we shouldn't have left, Cloe," repeatedly rocking back and forth as Chris put his hand on his shoulder.

The police asked questions about why we were there and what the hell happened.

We told them everything, they sent a rescue team to search but they found nothing and no traces of us being in there, and they asked what happened to Cloe. If there was an accident, they needed to know if we were covering up something. They asked us for anything, if she had fallen or got lost in the mines; if we had seen where she had gone; if we had made this story up, if something had happened somewhere else.

In the end, it turned into an accident and later into a runaway case since, without our knowledge, it seemed that she was getting ready to leave this place sooner than we thought. She apparently had written a letter to her father saying he wasn't going to see her again.

She hadn't told us any of this, but I thought back, and she had been hinting at wanting to have a huge dinner on the last day, that there was something important she wanted to tell us. If she was planning on running, she would want to tell us and the dinner with all of us, that was it. She wasn't running away, not from us.

The truth is, we never knew what happened to Cloe; not exactly, we knew that something was in those mines and that something did take her, Nate and I knew the truth.

Months passed and we mourned Cloe; our friendship was never the same again. We rarely hung out as a group and Nate was so distant, he said they boarded up the mine and put a fence around it so no one would be able to get in again.

A few more months passed, and we graduated, we all decided to go back to the cabin to say goodbye before we began drifting apart more and beginning college, and to say a proper goodbye to Cloe. Nate suddenly said he was going back to the mine. He said he swears that he hears Cloe calling to him. He said he went around the mine fence once and heard her voice clearly telling him to come find her, to help her.

I could see the painful look in his face, I didn't know what to say. As he looked for me to say something, I told him that it was a bad idea and that she was gone, he needed to accept that.

He seemed angry and left the room. Annie said, "Mai, don't take it personally, he hasn't been the same. I'm sure he won't do anything crazy. I think he just needs closure; you know. Plus, you haven't been the same either, you won't talk about it with us." She leaned her head on my shoulder.

I thought back, none of us have been the same; nothing was ever the same; we would never truly find closure.

I went to Nate sitting outside; I placed my hand on his shoulder, and he placed his hand on top of mine leaned his head on my hand. "She's there; I know it," he sadly said. "I should have never left her, I said I would protect you both and I failed, I'm sorry Mai" he said still holding my hand as he looked ahead.

I gave him a hug and kissed the top of his head; I knew what we had experienced was so surreal; it was like a continuous nightmare I still saw.

"I'm going back inside," I said.

I looked back at Nate. I hoped that he would never go back. I couldn't stand losing him too, I knew what we had both seen and began to get worried, I hope he never went back to the mine.

# The Contract

# The Contract

Whatever came out that night wasn't a friend; it was something dark and unnatural, and it wasn't going back.

I'm know that that asshole is out there even now, I know that he is there, probably still making deals with people just as stupid or desperate to have something change in their lives as we were on that night.

It killed my friends, and I know that now, but no one believes me. They all think I'm crazy that after all has happened to my friends those unfortunate accidents or just bad luck and that I had had mental breakdown, some sort of psychotic episode and that I haven't recovered so that's why I am here today locked up in this place...but I'm not crazy, I know what really happened to my friends.

"They say all the shit I keep saying it isn't real it is in my head, but I know what's real, but it is just that no one believes me and yeah, I know the same story as always, right!? I always say in every fucking weekly meeting." I yelled.

"Calm down," the Doctor said, gesturing to the male nurse, he moved towards me.

I sat up and began yet again telling the same story. "Alright, alright let's go back to that night, shall we? Maybe this time someone will finally believe me." I put my hands up sarcastically then began.

I remember all my friends as if it were yesterday; that night will never disappear from my mind and my poor friends Kasey, Joel, and Martie.

I'll always remember Kasey's pink and purple streaks in her hair and her half a Mohawk and dark makeup, her black nails, ripped jeans and an old t-shirt from a metal band and her military boots that looked perfect with her slim figure.

Joel, with his loose hoodie, shaggy brown hair, and black faded jeans with patches from his favorite bands all over them, and ripped skater shoes he was my best friend since grade school.

Then there was Martie, with her nose piercings and black hair down to her waist and she was in a dark denim jacket and ripped denim jeans, always wearing her army style boots to match Kasey.

We all wore similar clothes on those days, I guess, all of us misfits. I always think they should never have met their ends like they did, and we shouldn't have ever agreed to anything, but we just couldn't say no.

It was a Friday 13th coincidence, maybe, or it was just a bunch of stupid kids who were too bored and just playing with things that they should have never been able to get, but hey, you can get everything through the internet nowadays, so why not try something fun and exciting. We all wanted and needed our lives to change, each for our own different reasons.

My friends, all of us were into some crazy shit like voodoo dolls, black magic spells, and things we thought weren't harmful, like a few spells, minor hexes, and curses, none of which had proven to work by the way, so yeah, just harmless fun, so we thought, but fun it was for us, just a bunch of bored kids that never really fit anywhere trying to find their way.

But anyways, it was Friday, the 13th, and we had all been excited to hangout and were watching movies, drinking, passing the time, and yes, there were drugs involved.

Anyways, cutting to the event that would change all our lives forever, literally.... We had skipped classes that day and found an abandoned warehouse. There were tons of those in our area, which no one ever checked. They were boarded up or fenced but they were easy to sneak into.

We had decided to try a summoning spell and to call upon a minor Demon because well, why not. We had read some were like genies or something; they could grant you what you wanted for a small price so why not try it. Nothing ever worked before, and it was fun for us at that time to just have something of our own.

We knew it probably wouldn't work because nothing had worked before but for us on that day, everything changed.

We used things that held a meaning to each of us and began the spell harmless fun right, just something creepy for that night to stir things up and we were all hyped. We had gotten something called a blood spell from the internet with some instructions on what to do and we got right to it. Excited with what could happen, we mixed our blood with the items that had a meaning to us and threw them in the fire. We've never tried something like this before.

We said the spell, the whole chant, and followed all the instructions, but nothing happened as usual. We waited for a while, then still nothing, so we just laughed, drank some more, and we began calling it a night as midnight was fast approaching, we started packing up, and then just a little after midnight, a guy appeared from the shadows out of nowhere.

He was so handsome, like he had just popped out of a business magazine ad, I looked at him and noticed his eyes were a sterling silver they glowed in the dim light and his hair a shiny beautiful metallic vibrant color and it seemed to glow in the light of the moon. He was just wow, amazingly perfect, not a hair out of place, and he carried a black briefcase with him.

Alright, so yes, you must be thinking about this bullshit again; it never ends but he was so captivating and there was something unearthly about him, like he was from another world.

He walked casually up to us, very calm and collected and smiled as if he were greeting old friends. Then he spoke, his voice deep but unthreatening, "Sorry for the delay, Business as usual, these meetings can really run away from you literally." He chuckled. It sounded so nice and yet so eerie it made my skin crawl.

"So, then what can I do for you kids?" He smiled, checked his watch and looked around at all of us; it startled us and made us jump like we were coming out of some trance.

I'll never forget his smile. It felt so cold; it ran a chill down my spine. I looked at him, his shiny perfect white teeth were perfect like him I couldn't look away from him and I couldn't move he was mesmerizing. I was frozen in place.

My best friend's girlfriend, Kasey, giddily spoke, "Are you the genie?" She laughed drunkenly. "Cause if you are, I want lots of money enough, so I don't ever have to work, a nice house, no, a mansion, and an awesome car! I want to be so rich."

The guy looked at her and smiled "But of course, sweetie, who doesn't want that, right!?" "But first things first," he looked around at us all. "Before we get down to business, there are a few things that need sorting," he said,

"Then we could get right down to business, right, little lady?" He smiled and looked over at Kasey.

"Now would that be all for you, little lady?" She nodded and giggled drunkenly. He then handed her a blank sheet of paper. She giggled a little and looked at the blank sheet, turning it over to see if anything was there.

"Wait," I said. "No," I chuckled, drunk from too many shots and beers "Ummm, don't you need to take this down or something!?"

The guy smiled, his eyes shining, "Oh, I have a great memory and remember all my...clients" he smiled. "But contracts are always nice," he said, handing each of us a blank page.

I always look back at that night and think, why didn't I or any of us ask more questions, like why I didn't ask who the fuck he really was, where the fuck he came from and why he was there at all oh and of course, what would happen with our wishes or desires, if there were any consequences but I couldn't ask. For some reason, I couldn't ask what I wanted; there was a block; I just couldn't say anything I should have said.

The guy who we never got his name stood there after we all had our papers. He pulled out a sharp old looking silver-tipped pen and told us to prick our fingers and drop just a little blood on each paper. he said and stood there watching each of us do as he said, then said, "Because I am a fair businessman, I will give you seven years each and I will make sure you get everything you want." His smile seemed just as beautiful as before but just as chilling.

We all laughed, and I don't know what it was about him, but we couldn't say no. We did as he instructed, and all our papers were signed with our blood and then the papers just disappeared.

We all made our wishes, no they weren't wishes, our desires that night on what we wanted, just stupid things that we would come to regret.

The guy smiled again, looked at his watch and the papers and they disappeared. He looked at us again and just as quickly as he had come vanished. We had all made our desires known, unfortunately for us, he never quite specified that we needed to be extremely clear with what we wanted and that no matter what we wished, our lives were over starting that night, and they had become his.

So, then what has put me in here you ask well those dam "Contracts" Fuck the contract and fuck that asshole. The fucking contracts weren't an illusion at all; we all got what we wanted.

That's for fucking sure, of course, not exactly how we all thought or how we all wanted but we got what we wanted, nonetheless.

Kasey was first. She got the money, the huge house, her mansion, and an awesome car; all she had asked for. She didn't have to work ever again she was rich but all these at the expense of her family; they died in a horrible accident, and she was the sole beneficiary, so she got everything, through the family's will. She, being the only survivor, it ate away at her, causing her to slowly lose herself in her grief. She stopped talking to all of us; we couldn't reach her. She said she knew this was her fault and this drove her insane and she took her own life shortly after.

Next was my best friend Joel, whom I'd known since we were in grade school; he was like a brother to me, the way he died was strange and it was extreme.

He had always wanted to be a hero, have his face in the papers, and a Hero he was. He died rescuing some people and animals from a burning building, before he could get out the building collapsed on top of him, he never made it out and he was burned alive. He was the hero he had always wanted to be, but at the cost of his life. He did save lives that day, like he had always wanted; he saved a couple of people and their two dogs and a cat and when he went back to look for more people or animals, the building collapsed. They said he was a hero to those animals and the people he saved that day, and it was unfortunate that he had died.

Yup, died a hero alright for fucks sake, but he was burned alive during the process and crushed by a building, what kind of wish was that I'm sure not what he wanted or thought his wish would be.

Martie was next; she died on Broadway, where she always wanted to be and where she said she'd love to die. She died alright but not the Broadway she thought of, not the big star of any musical or show like she wanted. Instead, she died there on Broadway Station entrance, mugged by two thugs, and stabbed to death; not what she had imagined, I'm sure. Well, she was a star for a bit, her photo was in all the papers on TV, and the media wouldn't give it a rest. So yes, she became the star of her own unsolved murder. I'm sure this wasn't what she had wanted at all, not the publicity she thought she would be getting, the wishes or desires were fulfilled but at the cost of all my friends' lives.

Now as for me, well, I always wanted to be 'known to be remembered' and look, you all know me, don't you? I guess I did get some of what I wanted. I am known around here by people, people who know me as that crazy guy with that fucked up story and who never shuts up about it.

I will tell you, though, I do feel like dying most nights, but I know, of course, if I do die, he wins, and I won't be around warning others not to make the same mistakes I made.

Not like any of you are listening anyways, shit, I'm sure you all are thinking of some shit right now, something that can make everything worth being in this dump, something you think you need or even the stupidest things that come to mind and then getting out of here when your time comes.

"Okay, then the Doctor sighed looking at the watch on the wall the session is over for today. Please, go back to your dormitories" Dr. Spades clapped and motioned for us to head to the door.

"Oh, before I forget, Miles, someone is here at the front desk to see you," the doctor said.

I walked through the long corridor into the front desk area, and I saw him perfect as always so beautiful, and the glare of the lights seemed to make him glow like an angel. Picture fucking perfect as always and that smile still sent chills down my back, just like it had all those years ago.

"Hello Miles!" He greeted me as if we were long lost friends, I just stood there, numb, he leaned in as if to give me hug like we hadn't seen each other in such a long time, which was true; I hadn't seen him in years, but he haunted my dreams and thoughts every hour. He gave me a quick embrace, and I just stood there frozen. He hadn't aged a day and of course why would he have aged he wasn't of this world.

It had been so long since that night. I will always regret that damn night why did we ever try anything, why did it end up working and nothing had worked before?

He then leaned over my shoulder and whispered in my ear, "I'm here to collect." he said.

"I see you've pretty much had everything you asked for. People know you; they talk about you here. Isn't it so wonderful." his voice chimed.

I saw a nurse coming towards us, smiling with a piece of paper. A little blood dripped on the white tile and my breath caught in my throat.

"Okay, my dear boy, just one last piece and our contact is completed, and I would have given you what you wanted." I felt his chilling breath on my ear.

He turned around to the Nurse "I'll be with you shortly, my dear, business and all that you know how it is," he said.

She smiled shyly and seemed like a good person, and I couldn't move or say anything to her. I wanted to scream and tell her to run away.

He looked at me as if reading my mind "Tsk, tsk," he said and smiled. "You know, ever since you kids called on me, business has been blooming. I like it here, so many contracts to sign, I'm as busy as ever. I'm never leaving this place, and I owe it all to you kids."

He touched my shoulder, and I felt all at once; the weight of my suppressed feelings, all at once filling me, my insecurities, my loneliness, and all my darker thoughts all coming in a rush. It was so intense, I couldn't hold back, they crushed me like a huge, heavy weight falling on me that I couldn't lift off I couldn't come up from that weight I couldn't breathe. A small whimper escaped my mouth.

"Oh Miles," he said, looking all sympathetic. "You did good, my dear boy. Now one last thing to get you going and it will be all over and where you're going, this will seem like a pleasant dream.

"Now go on, my boy, they will remember you after this, like you always wanted. Well, at least for a while anyway." He chuckled.

I couldn't stop myself and I screamed. I screamed until my throat burned and ran down the corridor and crashed through an open window, falling to my death. I felt every inch of pain I had endured when I crashed to the ground, I couldn't' move, I only felt pain.

The last thing I heard and saw before my eyes closed was, two nurses said "He was a good kid. He was known around here, you know he would never shut up about that story; he was a sweet kid; I'll always remember him, poor kid."

"Oh, Miles, you held on, buddy, but I always collect all my contracts" he laughed and checked his watch and disappeared.

# The Writer

# The Writer

"Hey Doug, yeah thanks, I know it's been a while; you're right. No of course, I get it, and thanks for that." I gave a small chuckle.

"No, Douglas, I'm very happy, and not too much in my head; yes, I remember eating when I do; I know I'm sorry for that." I quickly muted my phone and gave a loud sigh.

"Yes, still here. Yes, I sure hope it will do well too. Yeah right, I know, I know you're only doing this because you care. Yes, I do know it's not in your job description." Another chuckle.

"No, please don't, I'm okay. Yes, I'll get some fresh air and no, I don't just open my window or step into my yard, I'll take Lucy, we will head to walk maybe get inspired." I muted him and put him on the speaker, his voice loud on the phone.

I look down at Lucy; she's sprawling on her back now, dreaming. I see her foot twitch; I smile and walk into another room, trying not to wake her.

He continued speaking. I went back to the room again and started petting Lucy and she woke up as I he kept speaking; I look at her she's my loveable husky, always by my side since she was a puppy.

I go back to the conversation" I'm listening yes, yes, I get it. Look, Mary comes once a week, throws out garbage and gets me some fresh food from the market, makes dinners most nights, and checks in on me. Though honest I don't .... Doug, DOUG!" I speak loudly.

"I'm fine, no need to worry, but you know what I'll get back to it. Don't worry, once we...Yes, I mean I will go get some fresh air with Lucy; that's what I meant. "I put him on mute again, and he kept talking.

Sitting in my living room now Lucy pokes her head in, does the cutest yawn and stretches, jumps on the couch, puts her head on my knee, and I smile as I pet her. I look down and think, "You're the only one that gets me and that's saying a lot." I smile. I sat there smiling then said "Wanna go for walk? Wanna Go Car Ride!? Go to the trails!?"

She jumps up and gives me a lick, wagging her tail excitedly. "Go find your leash," I say, and she runs out of the room. I give another sigh, remembering Doug is still on the line.

"Yes, I'm here; nope, didn't mute you; ok yes, I had to use the washroom; geez, I'm sure you didn't want to hear that. Ok, look, I told Lucy we're going out; she's getting her leash now, so you see, going out for some air. Right, ok, if I had known, I'd have done it sooner." I laugh.

"No, you're right, I get it, I know, and thanks again. What's that? Oh, right, yes, we'd love to visit then.

Right, of course no, no I hadn't forgotten, it's on my calendar, really it is, plus you know, Mary would have reminded me.

What's that, yes, I know, and if she had minded, I'm sure she would have told me. No, I know, I know, and you'll be the first of course."

"Hey, listen, Lucy is at the door, leash ready to go, and getting anxious and I'm just putting on my shoes" I nod.

"Right, you have a great day too, and I won't forget; we'll see you tomorrow, okay?"

"Yes, yes, you too take it easy. No, I'm not trying to kill you, honestly if I was, you know I'd do something spectacular, and it would be unforgettable; it would be book worthy." I laugh.

"Sorry, it creeps you out but that's what I do, right? Dougie, yes, I get it. Don't worry, it will be ready soonish. I'll see if I can even bring what I have so far tomorrow. So, you'll see I am doing something with this whole away from the city in seclusion deal we did." I spoke.

"Ok yes, I will, but listen, I gotta go. You said get some fresh air, right? Ok, ok bye, and thanks again." I hung up the phone, took a deep breath and exhaled.

I looked down. "Ok, let's go, girl, see what inspires us today or just slack off and relax!" I smiled.

Driving down to the local trails was nice; it was away from the small town at least thirty minutes' drive, and it was so relaxing. It was a nice drive, no traffic really; it was still light enough to walk, plus we knew all these trails, but I took a flashlight with me in case we ended up staying past the sunset.

We were on the island, surrounded by small, forested areas and lots of water and fresh air, which were very peaceful. Of course, there were some private properties around us, and I wasn't too far from the main city, just a couple of hours but it was a nice break from all the noise and the hustle bustle of people, and it really took my stress away it gave me clarity which I needed.

Some other walkers passed us. I nodded Hello as we kept going to the trail that led deep into the other paths and branched out to other smaller paths that not many people walked. We had found and made our own paths where sometimes we'd sit and could view some of the properties on their own private islands, their own piece of paradise.

This trail we were on was nice, it was rarely used, and I think only Lucy and I used it.

We began walking when I noticed a faint light across the lake where an old property had sat empty for years on its very own island, away from everything. It was a beautiful house with large windows, and a green roof with a welcoming porch to sit on.

Must be nice, I thought, to live in your own private piece of paradise, with no visitors and plenty of space for a dog to run around.

I looked over at Lucy and patted her head "One Day" I said and patted Lucy.

I kept looking at the house when I noticed some new things that weren't there before large boxes near the entrance and smaller boxes around the property.

"Well, it looks like someone finally bought the property, Luce and here I was saving for it; it looks like we will have to stay a bit longer at our current address." I spoke.

Lucy came towards me with a small branch in her mouth. She was as happy as could be wagging her tail it made me smile.

We kept to the trail; and reached a nice perch spot where I could see the house fully and the little island clearly. I went and sat looking at the property, wondering who had bought it after all these years, thinking how much they had bought it for and how much work it would be fixing things up, but then again, the house, though empty for so many years, looked well taken care of and what a nice property it was. I took out some candy and sighed. If only I could have bought it, what a dream it would be.

Its own little island has a beautiful oaked house in its center, surrounded by wooded trees and paths leading down to a small dock. I noticed several large boxes and crates at the dock area as well and some leading to the house.

"That's weird," I thought. "They must have rented something to have moved there so quickly." Some of the boxes were open also but I couldn't see anything inside, they were just open. "I'm sure people will be there to move those in the morning, as they were blocking some of the dock", I thought.

The sun had gone down; it was getting late. I looked down at my watch; at almost 8 p.m.; I looked towards the house. I noticed several lights going on in the house. I noticed on the side the large glass on windows you could see into the house but as the lights were coming on, I couldn't see anyone turning them on. Probably remote controlled somehow, I thought. But the house was now bright, and the inside looked empty; just a couple of moving boxes were all around the house. How strange, usually people put the curtains up first but whoever moved in didn't seem to care about privacy. But why would they, with no one around to see what went on.

The house lights made it look spooky and created shadows all around the house, yet it stood bright like a beacon.

I got up and called Lucy over, "Time to go, my love," I said.

I looked over to the island again. I was startled as I saw someone looking back. I lost my footing, almost falling to the side of the rock I was sitting on. Lucy barked; I looked back at her. "I'm okay," I said steading myself.

I raised my arm to waive hello, but the person was gone. The new owner, I suppose, was probably a very private person.

As we began walking back to the car, I kept feeling as if I were being watched, which was impossible as it was only me and Lucy at that time.

I heard her growling, looking back constantly. I picked up the pace, not sure why, but something made me feel uneasy and Lucy's growling didn't help. I felt a cold chill down my back Lucy growled again and barked, looking behind us, which made me jump and my heart race.

We reached the car, my hand shaking as I opened the door, and Lucy jumped in, still growling. "Stop, Lucy, it's okay, we're going home," I sternly said.

I started the car as we drove away. I thought I saw the woman from the island house. I looked back and saw nothing there. I calmed myself and began to drive home. I looked at Lucy and she seemed calmer as well.

Pulling to the house, I noticed Mary's car in the driveway.

"Hi Mary," I said loudly as we came through the door, Lucy running to find her.

"In the Kitchen dear," Mary said as I heard her giggle and talk to Lucy.

She was so sweet I walked into the kitchen, her gray hair up in a tight bun, her 5'3 frame chubby and sweet, reminding me of my grandmother, with her sweater vest, long-sleeved camel shirt, and long skirt to match made her look gentle and kind.

She says in a motherly tone. As she wiped her hands and says, "I see you eat most of what I left for you, that's great. I bought new groceries and threw out everything that was expired. By the way, I'm making dinner currently; I hope you'll have some."

"Oh, and please try not to let things go bad I don't mind coming out here to visit you both but it's wasteful if every week I come & throw out almost half the groceries I had bought you," she scolded me.

"I'm sorry, Mary. I'll try to eat more, and I'll try going into town to do some shopping myself. I don't want to be a burden" I said.

"You're not a burden, dear, it's just wasteful, as I said, and all you seem to eat is candy and chips; those I bring for snacks, not meals," she continued.

I listened to her go on about things. I chuckled a little. She is such a mom.

"Ok, I'm leaving you, my boy. Make sure you eat. Don't forget about meeting Douglas tomorrow, I'll message you in the morning to remind you," she said.

"Thanks again, Mary, and don't worry, I'm fine. I'll try making it to town when I can, and thanks for driving all this way," I said.

She walked to the door and to her car and left. I waved goodbye to her and as I was closing the door, I felt a chill down my back, like I had earlier. I opened the door and stepped outside. Looking around, I saw nothing, but I felt the chill of being watched. Lucy was still there, and she began growling and barking but I'm not sure if there was anything out there, I decided to go back inside and closed the door. Tomorrow I will be going back to the trails before heading to Douglas' house.

I headed to bed set my Alarm to 7am I needed to plan for the morning that I'd shower eat Breakfast then head to trails then we would meet Doug later in the day.

Morning came, we made our way to the trails and headed to the viewing spot where I sat on the rock, looking at the house on the island. I saw the large crates were still there and most of the other boxes I had seen the night before we had left. I had my binoculars, which I had brought with me, and I began to look at the house to see if there was anyone there.

It was like I was obsessed with seeing what was going on at that house; I just felt that something wasn't right, and I wanted to know what it was.

I was about to give up and leave when a strange fog began surrounding the island. I quickly took out my binoculars and looked.

On the other side stood a beautiful lady, her long black hair blowing in the warm wind. She just stood there looking at me, she was beautiful.... Was she smiling at me? The more I looked, the closer she seemed to get, extending her arms towards me, and drawing me in. I didn't notice as I walked closer to the edge of the cliff that I was going to fall; it was Lucy that woke me from my trance.

She barked and pawed at me which made me jump up. I lost my balance and fell to my knees right before the edge.

"Thanks, Luce," I said with a shaky breath.

I looked at the island again. The lady had a wide grin; her teeth looked sharp now. It gave me shivers; it was like she expected me to walk off the cliff! Like she was waiting for me to fall.

Lucy started growling. I put the binoculars on again and looked towards the house. The lady was still there, with a wide smile on her face, like she was waiting for something.

I was shaken and decided to head to Dougie's earlier than planned. I kept thinking of that woman's smile; it didn't seem right. Had I really seen sharp fangs!? I couldn't explain what I had seen.

I spent the remainder of the day at Doug's going over my new manuscript, but I couldn't really concentrate. I kept thinking of that smile and it gave me shivers.

I told him that I might be thinking of submitting something different. He didn't seem so happy, but I agreed to let him know when I would complete it and told him I would get working on this new manuscript right away.

We went back to the trails after Doug's, and I went straight to what had become my lookout spot. I seemed to be obsessed with watching the house, although I felt maybe I shouldn't be there, but I was drawn to this spot.

The fog was back house, this time it seemed to be surrounding only that small island. As I looked through my binoculars, there seemed to be others there, I saw the lights were on around the property and could see through the windows since they still didn't have curtains, yet I saw no one walking around but it was nice and bright and with the fog it made it seem eerie.

As I was watching the house, I heard a voice behind me that made me jump. It said, "Join us."

I turned around to see who had said that, and nothing was behind me, I turned back to view the house and jumped a little. There were other people, no, not all of them people but something more I could see, they were all watching me. I looked at each with my binoculars and was so shocked that I almost dropped them.

The four figures, each unique and strange in their own ways. This included the beautiful lady, who was more enchanting than before. I looked and saw the first figure who seemed to be floating in the wind, not touching the ground. Dressed in a gray trench coat and wearing a white blouse, black dress pants and shiny black dress shoes. The whole look was breath taking and seemed incredibly expensive. His shoes never touch the ground.

How was he doing that!? I looked at his face; flawless and handsome but the eyes were full black as night he had no pupils, just black like a great void. I looked over at the others. The next a man I thought, he or it wasn't a person, it was a dark shifting shadow with darkness surrounding it that made a form of a man suddenly, but then shifted back to the dark shadow. It was constantly shifting like it couldn't be still, it took a form of a man briefly again but quickly returned to a shadow, surrounding his whole body. When it shifted again, I saw his or its eyes stand out as a blue-emerald and a beautiful face. Then it was gone again, but the eyes remained. The next one scared me so much I felt like running away but I stayed and continued to look at it, its eyes an Amber red covering all corners, and its face distorted without lips, just sharp teeth showing like razor blades. A huge what felt like a sharp shiver ran down my back and it felt like nails cutting me. I moaned from the pain it felt sharp and painful like it was cutting my skin. I looked at it and it seemed to grin, showing its teeth more which made it scarier. Lastly was the beautiful woman smiling at me again her arms extended out to me, calling me to come.

A cold sweat ran down my back that snapped me back into reality. Everything told me to run but my legs. They wouldn't move, I called for Lucy, she was there in an instant and pulled my shirt, woke me up and I began running my legs felt pained, but I ran as fast as I could, practically sprinting to my car with Lucy by my side.

A voice in my head, not like last time but something different, something sinister, said, "Come to us, we see your talent and it could be so much more if you join us, be one of us. If you refuse us, you will be forgotten, and your potential will be lost. Such a waste that would be." The voice slithered in my head and made me panic.

I started my car and got the hell out of there. I was literally shaking; my whole body was shaking. I tried to keep the car from swerving off the road.

That voice haunted my dreams. I wondered who it belonged to which of the three entities those things were not human. I was pretty sure I knew which one made me shake with fear.

I didn't go back for a few days. I was too scared and frightened.

I stayed home and I ended up writing a lot during those days, like something had awakened and taken over; the ideas just couldn't be contained.

A week later, when Mary came, she did her regular duties, and I was in my office writing. She knocked and asked if I had eaten at all, as the groceries she had brought hadn't been touched. Suddenly, she exclaimed, "Goodness, what has happened to you? Have you not eaten at all? It also looks like you're not sleeping either, you look so tired. My goodness, dear boy, you must shower, get cleaned up, and eat. I'll make you something."

"What has happened!? You writers are all the same, you get stuck in your head. I remember the last writer that was here she was a beauty but definitely in her own head, what a tragedy that was."

She called Lucy, as she came; she gave a sigh of relief and said, "Well, I'm glad she's ok at least. My goodness, at least you haven't forgotten to feed her, right, Lucy?" she chuckled.

I looked up "I didn't know there was another writer here; Doug never said anything when he suggested I come here."

"Yes, quiet a long time ago, before your time when I was younger, I used to take care of her as well when she came here to write her stories; her name was oh gosh it's been so long it was oh yes Claudette Foster."

"Was?" I spoke.

"Yes, poor thing. It was assumed she was carried by the ties and drowned near the private island. They never found her body, but someone said they saw her jump off the cliff. You know, the one facing that beautiful house. It's too bad too because after her death, her books began to sell like crazy and now she's famous. Apparently, the royalties are going to her family members or so I hear but I didn't know she had any family."

"I don't think I've heard of her." I said, "But I'm definitely interested in learning about her and how she passed away."

"Well, I'm sure it's on the internet somewhere." Mary said, "It was quite sad. She was a lovely girl, very young when she died too. She just had her whole life ahead of her, but you should know her under maybe a different name...you know, I forgot what that name was; she had a different pen name. I believe she's quite popular even now."

"Anyways, dear, make sure you eat and take breaks; sometimes you need to take in the reality of life instead and look around instead of continuously writing and being at the computer and in your head. Take rest for yourself."

Mary gave her usual speech about sleeping and eating and said she had left dinner in the fridge to eat it then headed to the door Lucy and I walked her there and said goodnight.

I grabbed something to eat and went back to writing. I felt inspired.

As I was heading to bed, I grabbed my tablet and took it into the bedroom, and Lucy lay in her usual spot beside me.

I looked up Claudette Foster and there were a few names that came up, so I looked up Author before her name.

"Wow, she is popular and has quite a lot of books." I said, looking at the pages that came up with the usual thing's info about the Author. There was not much there, then a website caught my eye that looked like some type of conspiracy site. I clicked and read.

Author Claudette Foster, born May 20, 1980, died May 20, 2002, age, 22 off the coast of Tofino Bay. Pen Name Audette Francis or Stephanie Mins. Her body was never recovered.

She was an upcoming author who had one major-selling hit book, "Mirrors" released when she was just 17 but had been struggling since that time to have another huge book release, she had written other books after but none at the scale of mirrors. She was a bit of a recluse and kept to herself that not many people on the island remembered her, as she never came to town much.

There were pictures of the residence she had stayed in while here it was this house.

It was mentioned that she died tragically by what some believe was a suicide off the coast of the island, but others believe she had become much more and was out there still.

The police report showed that an eyewitness on the trails that night had seen her jump but when the police arrived, it had been too late, and her body was never found. They believed it may have been taken by the currents as they were strong during that time of the year and after searching for a few weeks her body never turned up.

A year later after her believed death, her publisher released a book that was her next big project, and it was a huge hit. Since then, a few more writings have turned up and they have done amazingly well.

The site mentioned how interesting it was that new writings kept coming up after all these years, considering she didn't have any relatives. Her only family member, her mother, had passed away when she was twenty-Two and no other family had ever been mentioned.

Now the question was, who had her old writings, why were they still being published, and had she completed these writings while she was still alive or was, she still alive? All the new writings and pen names being used were very similar. The few new authors with similar writing styles felt like the same type of writing that were named, and a question was, is this Claudette Foster? Where was she?

It went on to say that her suicide may not have been a suicide at all, but that she had become obsessed with something, that she had been acting strange on the rare occasions she went into town she was always mumbling to herself. Maybe there was someone as a secret partner? Maybe, she had become one of those reclusive authors who lives off the profits and is never seen again. If she did have a partner, were they the ones releasing her work? Had they had something to do with her disappearance, her potential murder or caused it? Her partner was never known by anyone or seen as she had always been alone.

The site went on to say that they had taken it upon themselves to see if they could find her.

They had blurry pictures of what seemed like her and some sightings after her death, and the site said it was her but that she hadn't aged a day since her presumed death...Another conspiracy?

I clicked on the pictures most were blurry but one I was left breathless. This was the woman on the island; it wasn't clear, but it was her, I knew it was her. The last picture was dated four years ago, and twenty-one years after her death, she hadn't changed at all she still looked twenty-two.

I swallowed. What was this...? Who was calling me? Was this Claudette the lady I had seen?

"Come to us, join us, be great, and become something beyond great" A voice in my head slithered in. It made me jump, and Lucy sat up, looking around as if there was something with us. She began growling and it made me uneasy and afraid.

I suddenly felt as if I needed to go check the house. I looked at the clock; it read 2 a.m. I shouldn't be going out but I'm not sure what came over me I got up suddenly Lucy was in front of me, growling. She barked loudly and got me out of my trance, I saw her blocking the door as if to stop me from leaving, what was going on.

I decided to try going back to bed and try to sleep and I made a note to call Dougie later today. I wanted to know why he hadn't mentioned the previous author living here and if he knew what may have happened.

Lucy jumped on the bed. I joined her, wrapped my arms around her I said, "I'll never leave you Luce, and thank you for always being my little rock, I love you" She wagged her tail and gave a big yawn. It made me laugh and before I knew it, I had fallen into a dreamless sleep.

I called Doug and we set up a meeting at his place. We drove there, and Lucy jumped out, tail wagging. It always made her happy to see Doug and this made me happy as well.

I knocked on his door and waited for him to answer. Lucy barked excitedly as he opened the door.

"Well, this is a pleasant surprise," he said. "You don't ever call just to visit so then how have you been?" He looked at me up and down. I could tell he seemed surprised at my weight loss and how tired I must have looked.

"Are you hungry? I could make us all a couple of steaks and potatoes," he said.

"I came to ask you about the house, I mean, the house I'm currently staying in. Did you know there was a previous author staying there as well and that Mary was also the housekeeper there?" I spoke.

He paused "Yes, I knew, and that's why I sent you there. I knew your talent would flourish, and it has. You've been writing a lot, haven't you? You have so many ideas, it's great, isn't it?" He spoke.

"Douglas, what the hell is happening to me? What are those things on that island? You know what I'm talking about, don't you!?" I spoke.

"I know about the others calling for you and I know you will join them eventually, but you have to make that choice yourself and I know you'll be great along with the rest of them. You're a rare talent and are meant to be great and I knew that the minute I saw you," he said, looking over at Lucy, who was lying down on the floor, "You have to let go of this life and the things that hold you here," he said.

"Can I take her with me? What will I become? Are you one of them!? How old are you really?"

He suddenly asked casually, "So are you hungry? I am so I'll put some steaks on the grill. "You're welcome to have some. I'll also make some veggies; I know you like that too." He turned on the grill and went to get the food, which was already prepared for three.

It was as if what I was asking didn't faze him, like he had heard it all before.

"How about some wine?" He brought out the wine glasses and filled them.

"Umm, thanks," I said, and I did feel hungry, and wine would help my nerves.

"It will be a hard change so I hear but if you're strong, you'll survive it," he said looking at Lucy, if you can take her. I don't know, I've never seen any of the others here or any of the ones I've met have a familiar with them.

"As for my age, I'm 201 this coming September; not bad, right." He smiled.

As I said before, no, I'm not one of them, but I have chosen to help them, and that's what keeps me here. Funny thing, this is my house but for all purposes, it's my great, great, great grandfather's house. He chuckled again and it passed to the family, which is me.

"What are they? What about the girl?" I asked.

"I'm not sure exactly but in all the time I've been employed with them, they always have a knack for picking talented individuals from all sorts of backgrounds and walks of life from all over world; it's like they sense something in you, and they want you with them.

They are like influencers incredibly powerful, each having unique talents. I honestly haven't seen two individuals recruited in the same era in such a short time." He let out a deep breath. "Why are you not

65

excited to have been chosen? You'll be great, and I know you can make a difference, you'll be able to live forever. As for the girl you'll find out soon enough so as I said I believe you will be great and that you should join them." he said.

I sat there in awe. How was this possible, I thought things like this only happened in books were they vampires? But this was real life and not a book. I looked at him, not uttering a word.

Doug continued, "Just you'll have to disappear and leave this world behind and enter theirs. I'm not sure how it all works to be honest." He continued, "I've been employed by them for over 160 years, yet I look like I'm in my late 40s. I'm not sure how that's possible either, he chuckled but it's great.

I believe they each have special abilities and because I'm an employee and so is Mary, we seem to age slower," he went on.

"I see great potential in you, but you have to let go of your attachments in this world. All your attachments, I know I'm repeating myself, but this is the only way" he looked at Lucy again.

I looked over at her as well. She meant so much to me. I've had her since she was a puppy and how happy she made me just when I had nothing, I had her when no one had helped me; when I had been lost, she had been there as my support; she, was she was my attachment!!

No, this can't be, I can't…I don't understand what's going on.

Doug looked over at me and took a deep breath. "So, then what will it be? Will you become the writer, the influencer you're meant to be, or will you struggle in this world until the end of your days?"

"What happened to Claudette Foster!?" I raised my voice suddenly without meaning to.

"Oh, as I said she›s fine. In fact, you›ve seen her, you know what I›m talking about, the one that called you," he said.

"So then? What will it be?" He repeated.

"You mean, what will I become? Will I be a fog person or have teeth as sharp as razor blades!? Be mutilated or mutated into something I don't recognize! Look, I want to speak to the leader of this group," I said. "I need to ask them something and I hope they answer me. I can't just leave. Not, not like this, please, will you let me speak to their leader?" I urgently spoke.

"Pretty unusual request but I'll set that up" he said.

"Hey, Dougie, how many people have you sent to that house?" I asked.

He looked at me "I've lost count, to be honest, but I know the ones that have made it are still doing great things behind the scenes in the world. You'll see once you join them."

After dinner, I bid Doug goodbye. Lucy jumped on him and gave him a lick. Doug said goodbye.

We got to the house, I was in a daze with so much information at once, and I noticed there was a note on the kitchen counter from Mary.

*My dear boy, now that you know almost everything, please know it has been a pleasure getting to know you & Lucy. I do hope things work out for you or for both of you.*

*I've left the fridge full, & I hope you take advantage, as you'll need all your strength.*

*Best wishes.*

*Mary*

I put the note down on the counter and there I noticed yet again that I would need all my strength. What did that mean, Doug said the same thing.

I looked at Lucy on the couch playing with her favorite toy. She looked at me, her tail wagging. I can't let you go, I said to myself.

I thought of other things that meant as much to me; my mother, she had passed years ago, I had estranged family members; I didn't know them well enough, and I didn't think of them often enough to consider them close, so they were not any attachment to me. What did that even mean an attachment? I had old friends I had known for years, but all distant now. I had no idea what I needed to do but I needed to speak to this leader.

I knew it wasn't the woman; she was too young and new, it seemed. So it was one of the other three that must be the leader and a shiver ran down my spine thinking of that creature I had seen with razor blade teeth.

It was almost midnight when my phone rang, and it made me jump.

"Hello." I said, my voice was shaky.

«He'll be there soon» Doug said, "There›s a bottle of wine in your fridge along with some Belgium Cheese and Crackers and fresh grapes, get those ready on the tray. Oh, and try not to stare,» he said then hung up.

I ran to the fridge got things ready I took out the wine and wine glasses I set them on each side of the small island and set the food on the serving Tray.

I sat on the stool on the small kitchen island and waited. I kept making sure my shirt was not wrinkled, and my hair was not messy. I looked over at Lucy, still playing happily.

"Appearance doesn't matter, I see you as you are and what you will be." A voice said across from me; it was smooth, clear and firm but had a friendly tone.

I quickly looked over at Lucy; she was asleep now and dreaming. I was surprised she hadn't barked or stirred.

I turned back around to see those blue-emerald eyes looking back at me, just the eyes and a cloud of darkness. They stared at me, the seat moved, and then a form appeared, and the darkness disappeared.

He had beautiful almond skin; his coat was black, and he was wearing a blue dress shirt & dark denim jeans and casual dress shoes. His eyes were mesmerizing.

He moved but I never saw the wine bottle move, but he had a glass of wine and was eating some cheese with crackers.

He looked at me curiously. "Peter said you needed to speak with me. Oh, sorry, I meant Douglas, as he's going by now," he said.

"Yes, I, I wanted to ask...what do you want from me and why me? What is this leaving attachment behind? I, I don't want to, to leave Lucy if she's an attachment, I can't leave her and you see, she's all I...I just don't want to leave her." I said with a shaky voice.

"Attachments you see can be many things; in living and in death, or undead for us but they are still attachments; it's whether you're willing to let them go to move forward or if you are to be stuck in these attachments that they hold you back and you on not moving, you must decide what you are willing to let go of." he said.

I swallowed a large lump in my throat, but I still didn't know what he meant.

"What will you give? What are you willing to let go of? "He said.

"You see, the change process is a tad difficult for most, even though I even had a difficult time controlling my urges when I first changed, and your mutt would cause a bit of, shall I say inconvenience. We don't like drawing attention to ourselves, and there are very rarely a few who can manage a familiar but again it's extremely rare and I have yet to know if you would be one of those rarities as I see your emotions are not as of now fixed" he said.

I got scared and asked. "What do you mean!?" I asked.

"Well, once you join us, or if you join us you will see," he said.

"So, was that all? You're just worried about what you will need to let go of? To each of us, it's different; trust me, it will become much easier as you get closer to joining us," he said.

"We will see you in exactly one week, you know where," he said.

He then turned into a shadow and disappeared; only his eyes were the last to go.

"Wait" I yelled. I still had other questions, but he was already gone.

The whole week, I felt inspired. I kept writing nonstop the whole week, like everything I wanted to say just came out. I made sure to take small breaks, eat, and play with Lucy a lot.

Finally, the end of the week came, and I had completed my new manuscript for my book after two long years of me working on my old script and struggling; everything had just come out and I had written it so easily. I went to see Douglas, he was already waiting for me, said he had been expecting me.

I told him how feverishly I had written and how my new story, which I thought would be a big hit, he seemed happy with that.

He gave me a new contract to sign. He said once everything was done, it was good to know there was security for when I disappeared.

I took a deep breath. Lucy was by my side; my head was killing me I hadn't slept in days. I noticed that she had been uneasy the past days. Like she sensed something was coming.

"Don't worry, Luce, you're always with me, I promise," I said and patted her head.

I bid Douglas goodbye, but he laughed, and said that I'd see him again, and shook my hand.

I meant to drive home but instead, with the moon high, I drove to the trails to the spot where I had been drawn to so many times.

I looked at the house on the island, the lights all on and I saw them there. "You're Claudette Foster, aren't you?" I spoke.

In my head, her voice chimed, "I haven't been that person for such a long time; come join us," she said with her arms stretched out and a smile on her face.

I looked at the others all there, and then I was drawn to the blue-emerald eyes staring at me on her left, but I couldn't see the rest of him.

"It's time." his voice was in my head.

"What, what form will...will I take, what will...will I look like?" I swallowed looking at each of them with their features all so unique.

"What, umm, what are your names, you umm, you never told me," I continued and swallowed again my throat feeling dry.

"The form doesn't matter, you become who you are meant to be and as you know, I used to be Claudette and now I am whoever I want. I'm free to be who I want but currently my name, Claire," she smiled so beautifully.

"Why are you asking these mediocre things? You're delaying the inevitable. You have already chosen I feel it and see it." his eyes looked suddenly like the ocean depths, now a darker shade than before.

"Relax," a voice slithered in my mind. I instantly knew who it belonged to. It said, "He is still human, so he has questions, not willing to jump just yet. Are you, young one?" the voice said and chuckled a little.

I felt as if I were being suffocated by a snake holding me in one place, this voice was like oil that slithered in my mind.

"I'll offer my name, young one, it's Caim. Well, for now anyway. Like the others, we tend to change often, our names and sometimes even our looks" he said, "we don't always look this good." his psychic laugh echoed in my head, causing me a bit of pain.

I looked over holding my head from the pain and saw him wave, I stumbled; almost falling back. It was the one with the razor teeth and grotesque face, his eyes Amber Red, I should have known.

He said, "Does it bother you seeing what you're seeing? Does it scare you that you might take a form like mine? Oh, you should be scared, I see you for what you are." Caim gave a toothy grin, which was even more frightening.

"Ye..yes, it does it terrifies me," I said, struggling to breathe my hands resting on my throat I thought to myself, "What if I am like you, I mean what if I become distorted like you? I don't, I...."

His psychic laugh was in my head, "Young one, you must learn to be nice to your elders. As for my look, I like it, and if you look like me, you'll always be happy and smiling. Plus, I think it's rather amusing, I for one hope you'll look like me, or who knows, a little more terrifying." Caim laughed.

That was incredibly frightening, it made my whole body shake and it made me want to leave, to run, but I couldn't leave, I needed to know what they were.

I heard a laugh in my head. "Is he really going to survive this?" Another voice chimed in, this one, clear and authoritative, it was dismissive with an accent sounding European.

I looked over and I knew exactly who that voice belonged to. It was him, the one dressed in an expensive all blue suit and white dress shirt that I could never afford and shiny black shoes, again he was floating in the air, like he didn't want to touch the ground at all.

"I am Mateo for now, and you've heard the rest," he said with such psychic force that it made me fall on one knee, like I was bowing to him.

I looked up; he was looking down at me with a wide smile, as if he knew it would happen, like he had wished it to happen.

"Enough!" A booming voice in my head made me jump and hold my head a shot of pain hit me.

"Make your decision, NOW!" the shadow demanded.

"I, I, I choose to join you, but I won't...I.

I won't leave Lucy; I'll go mad without her." I said in a trembling voice yet trying to sound defiant.

"Then you have chosen." He laughed, amused by my decision.

"What!? I....I don't want anyone to die or whatever it is you to so I can join you." I winced in pain, I felt as if something was being ripped away from my heart.

71

"I saw it in your heart, you had chosen long before you came," he said this as a matter of fact.

"Please, what's your name?" I asked, holding my hand to my heart barely able to speak.

"Kofi is my name, for now, like the others. as for your previous questions, the forms you see before you are what we want them to be; they are true to who we are; our true forms in a sense, but our gifts allow humans to see what we want them to, like Caim, who finds it amusing to put that mask on, but you'll see him as he really is soon enough, we see each other how we actually are..

We each have our own unique skills or gifts, whatever you want to call them, but I've said enough already so you know exactly what to do. No more questions and answers." He spoke.

I looked over at Lucy; she was sleeping; she had slept through everything, and I hadn't noticed how that was possible. I looked over at Kofi.

"Go on now, join us." Kofi's voice was more forceful, and the pain shot in my head again and my heart hurt as well.

"Now jump. You and that mutt jump together to link, and one more thing, you will keep her in line, or I will end her." Kofi's voice was forceful and scary, and I saw him lift his index finger then put his hand down again.

I looked over at Lucy; she was now up and looking all over the place, alert and scared, she seemed to sense something was off her tail tucked between her legs.

"Jump," They all said at once. I stood, went to the edge, and looked down. The tide was high and covered the rocks below, but I knew they were sharp and jagged rocks that the water covered.

Lucy barked beside me. I got down, put my head on her head and petted her head. "It's ok, girl, it's you and me, right," I said.

She licked my face but whined, scared like I was.

I got up, and Lucy stood beside me. I took a deep breath, "Here we go," I said.

We jumped together and crashed into the water hard. I felt my bones shatter. The pain was excruciating. I screamed, water filling my lungs and choking me. All I could think before I faded was, Lucy, what have I done, I'm so sorry.

When I woke up, the pain was so intense, I couldn't help but scream but it felt muffled. I was feverish, and I couldn't see straight my vision blurry. I felt as if I was losing my mind with so much pain and nothing eased it.

"This is the only way Hun," Claire gently said sitting beside me, "We have all been through it, you have to feel everything" she sighed. "You're doing well."

My jaw was broken; I was hardly able to speak. "Lu-" I tried again; I tried reaching for her. "L-" I tried with pain shooting through me. I felt tears running down my face. With my blurry vision, I couldn't focus, I couldn't see her.

I then felt a different type of pain, still sharp and painful but different than my own. Then I heard a distant howling, it reached me and suddenly pain shot right through me, different than my own but just as bad. I cried out.

"Lucy", I thought, "I'm so sorry." Suddenly, I felt a weak jab, like a cold nose touching me. I didn't hear a voice; I knew what it meant; "It's you and me" I felt it like a psychic voice but not a voice more like a feeling I knew what it meant. I heard another pained howl in the distance.

I whimpered, scared but a wash of relief came over me, I knew she was with me. "Lu..Lu...Lucy," I said, passing out again.

The next time I woke, everything was so clear. I no longer felt the pain I had felt before. I felt stronger, I heard everything so clearly, the birds, the noises of the house. I still breathed in the fresh air. I heard the voices clear in my head as if they were next to me.

They didn't hurt me anymore, they felt normal. "Welcome, friend," Kofi said.

"Yes, welcome to the circus." I heard another voice and a laugh, there was no pain.

"Cheers to you," Mateos strong accent came chimed in.

Claire was laughing uncontrollably when I heard her in my mind. Where was she? I closed my eyes, I could see her clearly running around, holding a dog toy on the lush grass, and she brought the toy to my face?

No, to Lucy's face. I was seeing through her eyes, through Lucy's eyes.

I sensed her and thought of where she was and suddenly, I was there. The light was so bright that it hurt my eyes.

"Oh," Claire said, "here." She handed me dark glasses; they made daylight look like night but had perfect clarity.

"You'll have to wear those for now while you get used to being in the light again," she said, her voice not in my head sounded gentle and sweet.

I looked down and saw Lucy running around happily, wagging her tail like nothing had changed. The sun wasn't affecting her. Why?

"Oh, because she shielded her eyes right away after she noticed it hurt" Claire said.

"She's quite smart; you know, she went to see you before you woke, she opened the door all by herself and jumped to float lightly beside you and she laid by your side. She's picking up everything so fast. I wonder how she will deal in the future; if she prospers and lives, it will be up to you to keep her in line, but I doubt that will be a problem; she's quite attached to you." She spoke.

I looked down and she ran beside me. I could sense her thoughts. No words, but I knew what she meant.

"She's been eating so much, and she's already drunk like two weeks' worth," Claire said.

"What has she been eating and drinking" I asked.

"Come now, young one, you can't be that naïve." Caim chuckled.

His voice was clear and no longer painful to me.

I looked down, Lucy touched me with her cold nose, and I felt "Thirsty/Hungry", a mental jab.

"Yes, yes Lucy, one sec, ok," I said. She jumped at me, licked her lips, and razor-sharp fangs poked out of her startling me and making me back up a bit. She barked stronger than before she jumped at me, and it made me back away from her completely, this was Lucy, yet it wasn't.

"Ok girl, let's get you fed," I sent her my thoughts, and her tail wagged happily, and she calmed down.

"Come," I said unsure of what her reaction would be. I looked into her eyes, and the rims of her iris were a golden color, her pupils serene, and it looked feral. We stepped through the house doors, and she was gone but no, I saw her sitting beside the fridge.

"Fast, isn't she?" Kofi said he was no longer a shadow but a man, his eyes Emerald Blue, still so beautiful.

He chuckled. "You flatter me."

"You can hear me? Right, I guess you can like you had before, I wanted to ask you what happened. I mean, what did I let go of to be here?" I spoke.

"Oh, a life was traded for a life. You see, your old life and your mortal memories of that time, not all but most, are gone now." Kofi said it so casually, then looked at me. "It's really a small price to pay like your first memories the feeling of your first love, feeling of loss, they were ripped from your heart along with some other human emotions, how do you feel about that?" he asked.

I didn't feel anything; it was like that life was not my own; it was the life of a person who was lost, lonely and always struggling to find their way in the world I didn't recognize this life it was someone else's life; their death not mine and it didn't affect me like it should have. It was disturbing but it quickly went away. I didn't know how to respond. I looked over at Kofi and I quickly changed the subject.

"How come I'm not hungry or thirsty like Lucy?" I asked.

"Oh, well young one, because your human cells are still adjusting and the hunger pains haven't kicked in yet," Caim said.

I no longer found him scary; he looked like all the others normal; I was no longer afraid of him or felt his mental waves intimidating me as they once had before. It was like just talking to a normal person, his eyes were Ruby red now they seemed to change different shades of red. He was handsome, looked to be in his fifties with a circle beard and a loop earring on his left ear, his head clean shaven he had light skin and not at all as he had looked before.

"What happened to your face? Sorry, not to be blunt but you looked so different, menacing and just scary as hell" I said.

"Oh, no worries, youngster," he said. "I like a bit of, shall I say, drama and a little fun from time to time, I get a bit of a kick scaring the new potential people but sometimes so when I get bored it's fun to see reactions," he shrugged and gave a chuckle.

I smiled. "Well, you sure scared me," I said.

I fed Lucy, and I felt a gentle nudge in my head of gratitude.

"Oh, you still haven't seen yourself in the mirror, have you?" Mateo said. With all that had been going on, I hadn't realized that he was right.

"My reflection will still show," I asked.

"Of course, this isn't a fairytale or one of those fantasy books," Caim laughed.

I went to the mirror; my skin was flawless; it was still light tanned but somehow it seemed different, no blemishes just smooth; my eyes were golden and serene green, to match Lucy not like the others at all; my hair was deepest black; my teeth seemed normal but when I checked further, they became razor-sharp, like Caim's teeth. It made me step away from the mirror, and my nails also extended and became as sharp as I desired, I was mesmerized by the experience.

I felt a mental jab and looked down Lucy, who was wagging her tail, anxious to show me something, I looked down, her eyes were like mine and her teeth were razor sharp like mine. I closed my eyes, and I could see through her eyes. When she looked at me, there was a dark shadow around me that I couldn't see for myself.

She then looked around at the others; each had darkness surrounding them, but each was a different color or shape coming from whoever she was looking at.

I looked at her. I couldn't see any of what she saw if I wasn't looking through her eyes, I told her to sit in front of mirror, and she did that. I closed my eyes and looked through her eyes. Her shadow was large and in the shape of a great wolf, it was glowing gold, and it looked spiked and feral.

"Interesting, isn't it," said Kofi. You can see through her eyes; this is a gift that you and her share. I wonder what else you'll be able to do together." He asked.

That had been five years since our new life had started. I had done lots since we had "died" I saw my books; my writings were as popular as ever. I smiled as I walked through the stores, Lucy beside me, no one ever said anything to us. We were able to come and go as we pleased and had come a long way with lots of discipline and training.

I was a writer; the writer I had always wanted to be in my past life and now was in my new life.

I had always wanted to be able to reach the world and now, with my gift, I was able to do that and so much more, I could influence and make others see the reality of what this world had become and inspire them to help create a better world.

Lucy would assist me in reading each person's emotions and auras and we had become a tracking team for the rest of our group to find people with potential to join us and to change the world for the better it was a long process, but we were up for the challenge.

We had left our old lives behind and now travelled like others, finding potential to help change the world for the better, to change the lives of humanity. I had learned that there weren't that many people with dormant potential that could become more, we weren't that many of us as many had a gift but Lucy and I we were trying to track the ones that did with our talent.

We now had forever, and we were going to find all the talent that we could so one day we could assist in making humanity better. It was exciting, a new adventure that we were on. We travelled the world and met the rare others with familiars they too like us on a path to change the world. Now using our new skills, we were making our dreams come true and helping along the way.

I never thought when I met Doug that my life would change so much and that I would be part of improving the world and that I would be able to inspire so many others.

I had thought that vampires or immortals as Kofi had said were these blood thirsty monsters made up in the movies, but they aren't, and we aren't.

We are the silent watchers and helpers behind the scenes of history, we can inspire and influence when needed all the women and men who want to make a difference in the world. We don't drink blood, though we do use it to sustain us when we first turn but other than that, we are relatively normal or as normal as we can get, each unique and each in search of trying to make a real change in this world.

# Blood Moon Part 1

# Prelude

Years wasted; I was so close. We were so close, I thought we'd find him this time. He thought he could throw us away like trash!? He was so fucking wrong, who did he think he was!? My anger consumed my thoughts in what seemed like every day and every hour.

I felt him and I smelled him sometimes too; he was like a wave of fresh earth mixed with the scent of fresh wood.

I could sometimes see through his eyes too but sometimes I think he wanted me to see. As once he was in front of a mirror with a knife. I couldn't see his face, I could never see his face clearly, but I could see his muscled body that sick bastard ran the knife through his chest and wrote my name on his chest without flinching, I saw him smile and then my name disappeared. I knew that I wasn't the only one that saw this, as Katie screamed and ran to me after that vision, but said it was her name on his chest, not mine. I told her the same, we figured it was a shared vision. That bastard was calling us it was a challenge to find him.

Katie said she had felt something else, like others waking or panicking, some just like us wanting him dead or angry others being called and challenged like we were. Some, she said, just wanted to be with him, like they needed him, longed for him.

I had a similar feeling like there were others, but I guess she was more sensitive to this than I was. But, in the years we began our hunt, I had learned to tap into her energy and had learned that together we were stronger, like he had paired us up for a reason.

We found that we had unique skills. Katie, one day trying to see if someone could lend us money, went to a guy on the street and asked if we could have money. I remember her telling me, "I just went to him, asking for some change or more. The guy stopped, gave me his wallet, and took out $1000 in cash from ATM!" He looked like a zombie. I told him to forget it then he snapped out of it like he had been in a trance. I said thanks, and he just walked away. I yelled and thanked him again, but he asked for what and kept going."

I was so surprised at what she had said I wondered if I could do the same.

We had never been athletic girls but now we seemed to be able move and to do and learn what we had never been able to do before. We quickly began watching a lot of fighting techniques as we decided we were going for the kill. This monster needed to be killed and we needed to be prepared. We learned tactical weapons training, defensive moves and practiced constantly. We also learned about firearms weapons; in case we needed them. We had no problem getting hold of the weapons we needed.

All I wanted was to track him down and tear his fucking throat out, just like he'd done to me and my best friend; he had left us in the woods, left us for dead and stolen our lives. I still had no idea why he did that and what he wanted, why we'd never been found, and why we hadn't aged in all that time we had been missing.

I had a life at twenty-one, I was, yes, still figuring things out but I had plans, I wanted to be a doctor someday. I had dreams but still, a life, nonetheless. It was my choice that would make me who I was supposed to be, but he didn't need to take that away from me, from us. He had no right I wasn't even supposed to be there that night, but I couldn't leave Katie. She needed me and I had felt it somehow, I had felt her calling, so I went to her.

# The Waking

I remembered from the first time we woke how confused we were, how lost, panicked, and scared we were. We hadn't known how much time had passed. We were starving but it was a different hunger. It didn't feel right I had looked at Katie she had woken at the same time. Her eyes, they were different, a bursting gold so beautiful and breath taking and her pupils a dark green. I could hear her thoughts; they were panicked. So many thoughts going through her head at once; like my thoughts panic, fright, confusion, hunger. Then it all stopped. I heard her say, "Lisa, what's happened to you!? Your eyes look so different." She wasn't far from me, but she wasn't near either.

"So do your eyes." I answered, "What are you wearing? That's not what you were wearing yesterday! Who changed you?!" I said that as the light began to shine down on us. My eyes and my head began to hurt.

"Same as you, your clothes are different too," she answered surprised.

I looked down, I was dressed in jeans and my favorite t-shirt, my jacket and hiking boots. They were all my clothes, who did this and how did they get my clothes it all felt very freaky, whoever did this seemed to know us which was odd. And Katie, she was dressed similarly to me, like we were hikers.

Her golden hair was tied in a ponytail, a bit muddy from our waking and digging ourselves out. My hair was the same way, tied in a ponytail.

What the fuck was going on obviously someone had left us for dead and we couldn't remember what had happened and were the hell we were. Why were we in the woods? No, it was a forest, surrounded by trees. Who had taken us and again why? I closed my eyes, and a quick image came to mind I could see our surroundings. When I breathed in the smell of the damp earth; lots of trees and a small brook not far away. I could see it when I breathed in, like a small map in my mind. I could hear something in the distance a road, maybe.

We were unharmed, but I felt different, and what I had just experienced was different, new, and scary.

Katie wasn't far from me, she stood up and was there in seconds. She seemed as surprised as I was at how quickly she had appeared next to me.

"Lisa, what happened, and where are we?" she nervously said.

"I don't know," I thought, and she answered, "I don't either."

"Wait," I said. "I never said anything. Can you hear me? I mean can you hear my thoughts!?" I said in shock.

I sat up and crossed my legs and took a deep breath. She did the same sitting across from me and I took her hands, not sure why we weren't freaking out more, it was like we hadn't just been scared out of our minds moments ago and like we should be having a panic attack, but we seemed to calm each other.

We had a conversation without saying anything. We were both shocked and cried about what was happening to us and how lost we were. We hugged each other; it felt good to have someone with me that I could count on.

We walked through the forest looking for a way out. With what I had seen Katie said she could feel a road was ahead the vibrations of one. We came out of the woods quickly, and we followed the noise of far-off traffic.

We stood on the side of the road and saw a car pass by. They didn't notice us; they kept driving. It was a white, rust-stained truck that had passed us.

"Let's get on the back. Come on, let's go," I said and grabbed Katie's hand. We ran after the truck and jumped in the back and quickly laid down, the driver never looked back, probably thinking it was a speed bump.

We made it to a small town and headed to a police station right away. We had nothing with us, no identification and we were a mess, but we needed to know what had happened and we felt panicked when we arrived at the station.

As we walked in, we weren't given a second look; of course not, we looked like a couple of hikers or college kids, which we were.

84

We walked to the front desk "Yes, ladies, can I help you?" A police officer said, not giving us a second glance.

We let the officer know what happened and she quickly called her supervisor after he talked to us, and we found out the cops had considered us dead or missing, leading to an unsolved case.

It had been five years since they had searched for us, and since then the search had been closed. They asked where we had been all this time, looked us over, amazed that we hadn't changed from the missing pictures they had on file. He looked over at us, surprised, and he then asked if we needed to call our families and again, where we had been all this time and why there had been no contact made until now.

We had no answers, so we were asked to fill out some forms. They gave us a medical check as they insisted. They also advised we stay and answer more questions but both of us said No at the same time, and it was like they listened without a second thought; they said we were released, Katie said it might be better to have them destroy anything on us and then suddenly the officer answered and said, "Ok" and did as she had asked.

What the hell had happened to us? They just let us go; no other questions were asked.

It seemed we had been frozen in time. We had woken up looking the same age we were when we disappeared, and we couldn't go home as we had no idea what was happening to us, and we didn't want to endanger our families. Plus, we found out our parents had mourned and buried us years ago. So, we were on our own now it was best not to worry them about our sudden reappearance.

That had been the first day we woke up. It seemed forever ago now and from then on, we had found our own way to survive to keep moving on our search for what happened to us.

## NOW

With our unique skills, we had learned what we could do, we had practiced and tested them and fought hard to perfect them but that had taken a lot of time and we had learned a lot.

The first time we used them, Katie was trying to see if someone could lend us money. She went to a guy on the street and asked if we could have some money. I remember her telling me, "I just went to him asked for some change or more. The guy stopped, gave me his wallet, & took out $1000 in cash from the ATM! He looked like a zombie." I told him to forget it. "Then he snapped out of it, like he was in a trance, I gave him his wallet and said hello to him, but he smiled and walked away." I yelled "Thank You!" But he kept walking and asked what for.

"Omg, what's happening?" I said, surprised by what she mentioned. I wondered if I could do that too. I should have been freaking out but for some reason I didn't. It felt natural in a way that I should know what was happening to us that we should know.

We ended up stealing a car and finding a nice hotel. I went to the front desk to try to see if I could do what Katie had and sure enough, I got us a free room and told the concierge to forget we were there and if they saw us that we were hotel guest and to leave us alone and that we could stay as long as we wanted. The concierge agreed.

It felt cool, like a power rush that I could do anything say anything and people would do it felt great, but it also felt wrong. I heard my mother's voice coming into my head. "You know this is wrong, this isn't what I taught you, why are you doing this?" I just shook my head and knew we had to keep going.

We hadn't eaten in what felt like forever; we were usually always hungry nowadays.

I remembered Katie back then in our old life; she was always worried she'd gain weight but now no matter how much we ate, we didn't change. So, we headed to the hotel's attached restaurant, where we enjoyed a delightful meal.

We ordered what we wanted. I ordered a medium rare steak rarer, lightly cooked, and surprisingly to me, so did Katie. I thought, "Aren't you not eating meat since..." Then I stopped; I forgot it had been years we had missed and that's probably why we were always hungry.

"I'm starving," she said suddenly, "I know what you mean; it feels like no time has passed, but it has, and right now I want meat."

"I can't help it; I feel like eating this gross, bloody meat," she thought back. But when it came, we both scarfed it down; the bloodied taste felt great. We ate another, then had a beer. Wow, it tasted great, but something was off about the taste; it wasn't quite right.

We didn't know what was off at that time, why the rare meat didn't satisfy us much, but we were happy that we were no longer starving.

We left the restaurant and as we walked out, I saw a group of guys outside who smiled at us. One of them came our way and started hitting on Katie when we were outside "Typical" I thought she looked at me and smiled she had heard me, of course.

The other guys headed back to the restaurant, but the guy talking with Katie was getting a bit too grabby. I was about to step in but noticed that Katie was handling it. When he suddenly pushed her back against the wall, she pushed him back and he went flying and landed on a car smashing the front windshield.

"Holy shit," I said, "What the hell! We got to go, omfg. What the hell just happened?"

Katie ran to him. He was conscious; she quickly whispered something in his ear and ran back so fast that it seemed like a flash. She said that she told him to leave us alone and that he should forget us, but right now we needed to go to get out of sight fast as she wasn't sure if anyone saw what had happened.

Amazed at what had just happened, we left and headed to our room. We stayed there, afraid of what someone may have seen and what had just happened, if we knew that the guys in his group may say something about us so we stayed in our room as we heard ambulance sirens and police sirens.

There was a knock at the door. I answered, and a cop asked if we'd seen anything. "No," I answered. Then he asked for our ID which we didn't have, so I paused.

Suddenly, Katie was at the door with two cards; they were hotel cards. She said, "Here's our IDs officer, you're going to accept them and move on, we were in our room after we talked with the guys, and we saw nothing we are not suspects." She spoke.

The cop looked down and he said, "Thanks, ladies. Have a good night and enjoy Nevada."

Thanks: we both said at the same time and closed the door.

"What! What just happened?" I thought. "What did you do!?"

"I'm, I'm not sure, I grabbed the cards & told him those are our IDs to accept them, and he did!" She answered and laughed nervously.

"You're crazy strong too." I spoke. Then paused. "Are we both this strong? I mean, we've never tested our strengths and we don't know what else this maniac pumped us with probably drugs." I spoke.

Katie seemed excited "Well then, we better find this maniac and see what the hell he did!" she spoke.

We sat quietly, scared, just staring at each other. We didn't know what to do; we had talked about it but the closer we were getting to tracking him down, the more fear we felt.

That had been so long ago, and since then we had been stopping at hotels and we had been travelling trying to find this person that had been leading us around the country but the first time we had heard him we had been laying on our beds when we heard a clear strong voice, "Find me. You belong with me. Now, test your strengths; you will need them for the trials, as I need only the strong ones in my pack. Some of you, I feel your rage, but you will see you're clearly the chosen; you belong with me; we will change the world."

We both jumped up and looked at each other. "What the hell was that?" I spoke.

"I, I think it was him, the guy who turned us into whatever the hell we are." Katie said, hugging herself like she was cold. We had decided to try and sleep; we slept beside each other that night, and then as we lay there, we decided we needed to find him no matter what.

"Test, trails! What was this sick game for him to test us? What was this about a pack he had mentioned? What does that mean? What the hell mess were we in?

"I don't like this at all, Lisa. I honestly just want to go home and go back to sleep to go to school and graduate. Just leave this nightmare behind us," Katie said.

"Me too," I said, "But it's obvious we can't; we have to put that bastard down; see why he did this to us; and we have to figure out what else we can do before we meet him; we have to train in fighting techniques; we need to be ready for anything, you know this, right? I spoke.

Katie nodded. "I know," she said.

We decided to begin training more than we usually did so the next day, we decided to be more focused, test out our abilities and then begin tracking this guy.

I felt we were close to finding him, we had been testing our skills these past few years now trying to perfect them, but we needed to do more.

We got up early, hiked the hills near the hotel we were currently staying at and found a spot. "Okay, let's watch some videos of hand-to-hand combat." I spoke.

"Sure, what should we watch?" Katie spoke.

"Well let's see anything should be fine but honestly, I doubt we can learn much more, even though there's no deadline to find this guy. There's just so much to pick up but sure, let's see what we can find and see what we can pick up." I spoke.

So, we started watching the videos and started trying out the moves, and surprisingly we did well when we spared together. It was crazy; it's like we picked up everything so fast in a few hours that we had come from not knowing much of anything to knowing so much.

"We should try out others," Katie said.

I laughed. "Seriously, we've been at this for a while now, watching videos and practicing. If there are others like us, they aren't our target; it's that monster and we don't want to start something with others, plus honestly, I don't think others can handle us." I gave a laugh.

We trained like this for a few more days of hand-to-hand combat but then I had a thought, which Katie agreed with immediately.

For our next learning lesson weapons training, we looked up videos and learned what to do with hand-to-hand weapons training like knives and then we went to a shooting range, and it was amazing we both shot perfectly, the range manager asked if we were from the army, as he hadn't seen anyone load and unload guns that fast and how knowledgeable we were. We told him our fathers were in the army and had taught us how to maneuver weapons.

At the end of the week, we had new clothes, and we were ready to go hunting for this maniac.

We had learned so much in such a short time, and we would always practice on our spare time. We didn't know where we were going or what we were about to face but, in a way, we knew without knowing that we had to go.

About a month passed and we learned so much about our abilities and what we could do. And again, when we thought we were getting close, he would disappear we couldn't sense him. It seemed we were being led to a remote location far away from everything.

We had been sensing different smells around us but, in a way similar, we had also had several more shared dreams and each time we followed the directions it told us, we constantly trained and learned that we could create a solid shield around us. We had found this out when we practiced at a batting cage once, and I let my guard down when Katie yelled, "Watch out." I put my hand out to protect myself, and the ball bounced off something solid, then hit the ground with force. It broke in half!

"Omfg," Katie yelled excitedly. "How did you do that? That's so crazy wicked, I got to try it!" She went to the pitching machine and stood there, ready for the ball to come. "Wish me luck!"

Then she closed her eyes and before she got hit, the ball bounced back but remained in the air. She opened her eyes and put her arms down then the ball hit the ground hard. It broke the same as what had happened with mine but hers exploded.

We began to train more, using our newfound abilities, to see what else we could do to learn and use for the upcoming trials.

Finally, after another few months, we made it to the remote location he had led us to. We were carrying backpacks with food, water, and weapons, and anything else we thought we would need or that we could help with this whatever we were going to do or thought we were doing.

Katie kept telling me she felt others stronger now than when she first had and sensed them, and she heard them sometimes like whispers in her mind. I told her I felt them as well but not like she did. I only sensed their presence here and there, but I never knew where it was coming from or heard them like she did. We began to head into a wooded area that we were being led to.

It was a quick hike for us, no trouble at all. We had been training all the time with our new abilities that we now controlled and had practiced. We had fighting skills weapons training; we were a walking arsenal, and we knew how to use everything at our disposal. We had prepared for everything that we thought would come our way or so we thought.

"Remember, stick together and be on guard," I said to Katie, she nodded.

When we made it to the clearing at the top, there were several others in pairs, just like us, already waiting. Most had bags or backpacks like us; they also seemed prepared; others were just there, standing and looking around; and some just seemed scared, others were shoving each other playfully having a great time.

"I can't wait to see our host and rip him apart," I thought.

Then I noticed that some of the others there looked our way; could they hear me? I looked at Katie and she shrugged.

"Yeah, loud and clear, princess," someone with a deep voice came through in my head.

Another chimed in, "Don't worry, I wouldn't let you get near him, and you risk breaking a nail." Another chuckled, "He's all mine."

I didn't know who had said anything. I looked around at all the faces around us, trying to find out who had said this to me. I looked around at the scared and fidgeting people, as well at others who appeared angry and pissed off. Then there were the few who seemed happy to be there, laughing and joking around like this was all fun.

They were from all different age groups, races, and nationalities; I thought I saw a kids and teens in the crowd. Others looked psychotic and wild, each of their eyes looking towards us, and each seemed to be scanning the area and sizing each other up.

A quick thought crossed my mind. Then I heard "Judging isn't nice, little girl," a women's voice said this time.

Then a deep voice like an ice sent a chill down my back and said, "You and that other whore will die tonight." A laughter that sounded wild and crazy answered her.

"Try us if you think you'll survive, asshole," the same woman's voice answered.

Then more voices all at once came, saying different things, some challenging each other or us and some softer ones but still loud; saying they shouldn't be here, and they wanted to know why they were here. Then I heard small voices that sounded young, just kids saying they wanted to go home and see their families, some crying and other voices trying to calm the younger voices down.

"Why the Fuck Don't You Say It Our Faces?" Katie yelled suddenly, making me jump. "Come on now, you ass holes! Why don't you just step up? We're ready; show yourselves!" she continued.

I grabbed her arm to calm her down and looked at her sternly so that she knew we shouldn't start anything with anyone.

That got a laugh out of the ones. I could see in the clearing and a few at the back.

"Enough," a booming voice that dropped most to their knees and brought immediate silence to everyone, boomed out of nowhere.

Sudden pain shot through me like a barrage of cuts deep in my skin. I looked around and saw others fall to the ground. I was determined to hold my ground. I stood as many fell to their knees, determined not to fall holding on with all my strength. The pain was so strong that it made both of us wince and made me dizzy. That's when I felt Katie, she was about to fall, but I shook my head at her. I saw tears in her eyes, I let her know we would not fall, we would stand together. I grabbed her hand strongly. She looked at me with her golden eyes in pain, but she held on and nodded at me. We stood through the pain that rippled through all of us. The pain seemed like it went on for hours and then...it stopped.

"Well done, the lot of you." A laughter came out of nowhere again, with a loud clap, echoing through the area, and he continued "Looks like an interesting group this time."

"This time? What did he mean by that?" I wondered.

The sudden release from the pain took my breath away. I felt a sense of relief that I could stand again and breathe normally again.

I looked up at where the voice came from, my eyesight still a little blurry. I saw him. He stood tall, a handsome man with sandy hair and silver eyes. His body looked strong, and his muscles were showing through his shirt. He began looking around at the group.

"This is amazing," he smiled, his shiny white teeth and sharp incisors showing. He took a deep breath and took another long look.

He smiled and nodded to himself as if he were so proud of himself of that he had done to all these people, as if he hadn't taken their lives.

His smile gave me chills. I wanted to run but I also wanted to smack that smile off his face, I looked at Katie and she seemed to want to do the same.

He continued, "Today, ladies and gentlemen, will be the start of a new life for the next couple of weeks, days or maybe even hours for some of you; you will become so much more."

He paused, then continued, "For you see, in the next couple of weeks there will be a new moon not just any moon but a rare moon and soon this is where whoever survives and yes, survives will become part of my pack."

The strongest will be welcomed as my Moon children, blessed by me. This is where you will become stronger and gain a family, a true family." He smiled and held his arms out as if welcoming us, looking at everyone, and suddenly felt like he was about to eat us alive.

I felt Katie's panic. I held her hand and I suddenly found it hard to breathe again. I looked around, I wasn't the only one. They had felt the weight of his presence.

"Well, now let's have some fun, shall we?" He gave another loud clap, it startled us all.

"As you can see, you're all in pairs so hope your partner is strong or it will drag you down and you'll lose the game, shall we say. Since that sounds much nicer than what it really is, isn't that right so we shall call it a game.

So, if you die well, your partner will have to find someone new and vice versa. I do advise you to find a new partner or see if you can make it on your own if you think you can but that may not be so easy," he smiled.

"Oh, and just a small warning, no leaving, as I will end you if you do. Okay?" he said so casually as if it were nothing.

"My only goal here is to find a strong pack to have the strongest pack and to bring those who pass and survive a new life a better life to eventually make a new, better world."

"There are, of course, different challenges that you will all be dealing with and if you're strong, you will do well. You'll be tested on many things, like your mental and emotional strength, physical strength, and of course, test of will and cunning, which will play well in this game of mine, of course. Your skills each of you by now should have noticed that you or your partner possess certain unique traits, will come in handy for survival."

As he said this, he smiled, his handsome face suddenly turning to that of a Grey Wolf's head, showing his sharp pointed teeth, and his eyes went from silver to sterling grey. It was scary as fuck.

Suddenly, in a voice, loud and trembling, someone said, "We never wanted to be part of this; we want to go home, my brother, and well, we just want to leave. We never asked for any of this; we ask for you to let us go, we won't breathe a word to anyone, we promise."

Another voice, a much younger sounding voice came through, "Our grandparents need us, we are all they have; we left yesterday, they must be worried, you see."

I heard a bit of laughter and snickering. A group made way for the speakers; they parted ways for them. I saw them; they were so young, maybe in their teens, 14 or 16 max. It made me so mad but also sad. At that point, I began to rush to the ass hole in the center, but Katie stopped me. "Don't get in the way, we have no idea what he can do or what will happen. Plus, you've felt it that some are already aligning; with him you've felt it since we got here, haven't you?" she whispered in my ear.

I nodded, stopped, and turned back to see what was happening. I heard him say, "Well, as I was saying when I was so rudely interrupted, let me continue. My name is Jax and I'm thousands of years old so yes, I'm strong, and you should all be grateful to be here and to have been picked to be part of my little experiment. You will be the first of many to change this world to create a new world and I will be your leader in this new world. You will be my children, the children of the Moon, but also so much more. You will not just be a strong force in the world where you will learn so much and change at will; you will see what I mean if you survive, that is." He continued without missing a beat; he was at the center with both brothers now. I never saw him move; I heard gasps, then someone screamed. He was holding both brothers by the neck, and he threw them at his feet.

"Boys, boys, boys, your grandparents are long dead, and it's been 5 years. Geez, check the papers much." He chuckled, and a few joined him nervously. It was so scary that a large lump formed in my throat.

I never saw him move. "Katie, how did he do that!?" I whispered.

"I didn't see anything either; he was there, then he wasn't?" she replied.

"Silence my pups while I continue," His voice again began booming, hurting my head again.

Everyone went silent right away.

"Okay boys, I'm going to let you go home to show everyone the type of guy I am" He smiled, but when he did, it felt threatening and scary.

"I did earlier say there was a way to leave; perhaps you missed it, maybe too much in your thoughts? But anyways, I'll tell you, just go south of this clearing. There is a town not far as I'm sure you noticed coming here so, please go. You should be able to make it before nightfall. Now remember, be quick. You wouldn't want to get lost in the woods. Oh, and boys, you can always find your way back to me." He smiled again, looking menacing and dangerous.

The boys stood and grabbed their bags and looked at the others and at Jax. "Thank you, Sir," one of them said swallowing.

Someone in the crowd said, "Don't," but they began to run so fast that they disappeared within seconds.

Katie let out a breath she'd been holding. I heard her voice in my head "Those were just kids; they deserve to go. I hope they make it." She looked down, her eyes closed, hands to her heart.

I was looking at them disappear when I turned towards Katie to grab her hand. I heard a scream in the crowd and mental panic from all directions, what was going on then I heard someone, "Holy Fuck! When?" Someone exclaimed.

I turned and looked at the center; the boys' dead, torn bodies were there! He had their hearts in his hands.

It made my stomach turn and I wanted to throw up, and I felt Katie grab my hand.

"Now, ladies and gentlemen, this is how you exit the pack in case you missed it. I did say I'd end you, though I would rather not, but anyways, so then you will fight strongest, survive, and we create a new world. That's the just of it." Jax said casually.

We were split into groups, but we would be competing against everyone as he had informed us to get a head start groups would be sent in at different times. No time was specified. This reminded me of gym class, where we were placed in groups and supposed to compete against each other, but this wasn't a competition and some of the people in our groups would not make be getting out ever.

The winners would move on…. but move on to what exactly, that's what I wondered, all I knew was that we needed to get through this and that we were going to make it.

We were separated into groups and ours was made up of ten people. Two Burley guys; they looked dangerous; their chests puffed out, they weren't carrying anything, but their appearance looked intimidating.

Two women who looked about in their 30s; they seemed tough but had nothing with them no bags or any weapons I could see but who knows they could have something.

Two guys around our age; from what I could tell, maybe a little older probably in college, they had backpacks like us and rifles.

Two other women as they looked in their fifties but in good shape, I noticed a gun on one of them.

And of course, us, making a group of ten.

We all looked at each other, no one said anything or thought anything. They were keeping whatever they were planning a secret we needed to be careful.

Our host informed us that he would want to get as many survivors as possible from each group but understood if that wasn't possible.

If your partner died, it would be up to you to find another partner, team up with others but to watch who we trusted, or you could try making it on your own but remember that this was a survival game, so do not be too fast in trusting others. He seemed to be trying to make everyone uneasy and paranoid. He also reminded us that he would be watching the outcome and said he hoped we would all be entertaining to him as he wanted to see a good show and who was stronger.

He smiled again but now we all knew that he really was, and it seemed to make everyone uneasy except the ones who for some reason, seemed to be so taken with him and still craved his approval. Those I believed were the most dangerous.

"We will begin trials in the morning." He continued, "Get rested from today's excitement and get ready for tonight there are no rules other than to survive. If you get killed during the night, then, oh well, think of it as one less team or person to compete against, right?" He smiled again and looked excited. "Have fun" he said, "Oh and remember no one leaves without permission." He disappeared; he gave us a reminder again that no one left without his permission.

It started getting dark fast and everyone was there, so many people. We had our sleeping bags and a tent; we looked around and spotted a clearing on a rock away from the crowd. We grabbed it fast and set up camp. We placed motion detectors around our tent. We had decided to take turns guarding.

"Sleep tight, kittens," someone said it sounded like one of the guys from when we first arrived. I looked over and saw another guy blowing us a kiss.

"Gross," Katie said.

"Ok, we will be fine. Remember, we got this, we trained for this." I looked at Katie, trying to reassure her. She was shivering. "Hey, Katie, we got this," I said as I grabbed her hand but honestly, it was more to reassure myself. I was just as scared as she was, but I tried not to show any emotion and not to let my thoughts wonder. Katie gave me a hug and went into the tent.

Katie slept while I stayed up watching our backs. I knew my eyes would adjust to the night. I held my Taser Gun as I watched some of the others set up and begin to sleep. I heard snoring near us, I set a timer like we'd agreed so we could each get rest.

Katie was sleeping restlessly; I could hear her jumbled thoughts.

During the time I was up, I watched and cleared my thoughts to try to really listen to what others were planning. Most were thinking of taking out some of the weaker looking teams. There were a lot of thoughts about Jax and most seemed intrigued by what they had seen, and others had some excitement, which was very unsettling. Those were the ones that we hopefully would be able to avoid.

Others were talking to each other, thinking of plans and making alliances and then there were the ones who were thinking and talking about ways to escape without getting killed; those were the ones that could help us, I thought.

Hours passed like this with a lot of voices planning and plotting, then finally it quieted down but there were still a few up still plotting, I couldn't tell where they were, but when they began taking each other out, it was very clear by how quickly people started becoming quiet and just disappearing the fights had begun.

Then the noise began. The commotion woke Katie up, she was still sleepy, "What's going on," she asked still half asleep.

"People are killing each other," I said in disbelief. That woke her up right away; she grabbed the knife beside her and was right by my side. We saw someone rushing at us "Ok, this is what we practiced," I said, and we stood back-to-back and held our ground. I tased someone, and Katie did the same. We kicked the tased guys off the rock. We kept fighting, holding our ground. I was tired from a lack of sleep. "Don't worry, I got you," I heard Katie's voice in my head. "No, don't." I told her not, yet I can keep going. "We can't, not here" She nodded and knew what I meant. "Okay," she said.

We smelled blood in the air and saw lots of dead bodies around us. It seemed like half the people had been cut down, but we were still standing. People were just going crazy. I saw a fire blast and icy spikes, the earth opening, and a boulder floated and came crashing down on someone. They tossed it back to whomever threw it like a ball.

There were so many screams; so many cries from the younger groups, it was a blood bath and it made me sick.

Laughter came from nowhere and suddenly it brought everything to a halt. "What a glorious sight," Jax beamed.

It knocked us to our knees this time; the fights ended immediately, followed by silence. This time everyone fell, and we couldn't stand like last time.

"Perfect, perfect, this is enough; yes, the weak have been cut down for the most part" he said. "Oh, and I see there will be some new pairs to be made" he continued. I looked at him, he stared back at me, holding my gaze. "Ok, I don't do this often but I'll give you a gift since well you all are my first of many that seem successful. Tomorrow is a new beginning so then SLEEP."

His voice rang in my head. I looked at Katie; she held my hand, then we passed out.

# Blood Moon Part 2

# The Beginning Of The Trials

"Lisa, Lisa, wake up, wake up." I heard Katie, as she shook me awake.

I woke up, I wasn't in pain, I felt rested, and I wasn't hungry.

"What happened?" I asked her to take a look around to see where we were; we weren't at the clearing anymore.

"Katie, what happened, and why are we dressed differently and cleaned up? Do you remember anything? How long have you been awake?" I just blurted out so many questions.

"It's okay, relax," she said. "I haven't been awake long, maybe a minute or so longer than you. As for your other questions, I'm not sure who dressed us and cleaned us; your guess is as good as mine, and I have no idea what happened. Yes, I'm not hungry either; it's a little strange considering we haven't eaten in almost two days," she said.

Our backpacks were there beside us, we quickly checked them before deciding to go. Everything seemed to be there; nothing had been taken, and nothing was missing.

"Let's go," I said. Before we left, I looked at Katie and nodded and closed my eyes. She grabbed my hand and joined me. We started by mapping out the area, it was like a huge maze. We tried pinpointing people; we could only see two groups near us; we needed to stay clear of them.

Yes, we had tricks up our sleeves; we hadn't yet shown all our hands; we had only done combat and some of our weapon's skills, nothing else, as we had decided not to show what we could do until we needed it or if we were alone like now.

We decided to avoid the groups around us until we could get out of this maze-like forest and find the exit. We heard fighting and yelling but we always tried to go a different way if we could. So far, this seems to be working for us. We had decided to stay away from all fighting only if it was unavoidable would we fight and so far, it seemed like we might have to.

We ran into two pairs, but when we ended up fighting, they weren't too tough, and they didn't rough us up too much. We didn't kill them, but we knocked them out and kept going.

We kept running thankfully into weaker teams and some when they saw us run away it seemed they were also trying to avoid fighting as much as we were.

We stayed in the maze for a few days avoiding the fights and trying to get out we again mapped out the area. I saw there was an exit not far away, which was great. It had been four days already and we needed to leave. Katie got excited, and we concentrated on seeing if there were others near that exit. It seemed we weren't the only ones that found the exit; other groups were moving there too and fast.

We saw two guys from what we could make out standing at the exit, like blocking the exit.

"Get ready," Katie said. I sense that these guys aren't waiting at the exit as a welcome party; they are eliminating people that come through so then shoot guns and shields up?"

"Yes, but wait for shields and the rest, we don't want all our cards out" I said.

"Kitten, is that you? So, bossy to your buddy there, kitty. Let me guess, who's talking and being all bossy; the kitty with the black hair, tasty looking flesh I would love to just cut into. Don't you think you should stick together till one goes to heaven or if you're lucky, both will go to heaven together, but it will be hell first; my name's Vince, by the way," he said.

"Here, kitties, kitties come out and play," he laughed.

"Hey V, let me get em," his buddy said, "We already got the other ladies; they were no fun and died too fast. I really want them they seem fun, oh, and those other kids' fuckers were fast, but they won't make it through here," he laughed maniacally "I want to hear them scream those stuck up..."

"Enough," Vince yelled "We got em'; they can't get through here not without dying first."

"Did you forget there's more than just us out here...Vince, was it? Who's your buddy?" I spoke.

Katie looked at me as if to warn me not to egg them on. She put her finger to her lips, closed her eyes and put her hands out. I nodded and put my hand on her shoulder. She took us to see where they were it was one of our skills we had discovered I could map things and she was the one that could take us to see what was there before we got there it was extremely handy and had gotten us out of bad situations in this so-called game.

We saw them standing at the exit and a big, burly guy was there; Vince, I was sure, and I think I remembered him from that night before we had been placed in the maze and the other guy pale and skinny he was constantly moving about his partner, I presumed.

Ok, so we knew that from our group, at least 4 out of 10 of us were dead. As for the others, I had no idea who they were; they hadn't been in the group we had been in. We sensed more people coming from other directions.

We had a few unavoidable fights, but luckily, we had seen where they were, so we had been able to avoid most of the groups but some we had to fight, and we had come out on top, but it sickened me to think of what we had done to make it this far leaving them alive but barely in some cases. But I do remember the ones that had fallen by our hands, how we had hesitated but, in the end, we had done what needed to be done, and because of this, we would never be the same. It made me angry that we had played his game.

Now we were here, almost at the end "Hey Vince, we see you," I said as I aimed my rifle at his chest and fired.

Katie flinched and she nodded. I had hit him straight on, and I knew I hadn't missed since we had been practicing.

We looked again; he seemed to be standing there like nothing had happened, but I noticed a figure I couldn't quite make out; it was a person he threw them on the ground. I had shot one of their allies; they were dead. He turned to face a lady; whose partner must have been the guy I had just killed. "Sorry, darling, you're no use to me. I saw what you can do; you're useless without him," he said, and he ripped her neck open, kicked her to the side. She lay there bleeding out, her body convulsing, and then it stopped; she was lifeless, she didn't heal, seems she must have been connected to her partner.

This guy was crazy; he had killed his allies like nothing.

Katie put her finger to her lips again. We concentrated on hearing others were saying some thought Vince was unpredictable; he needed to go; others were thinking; that they should ally with them; others wanted to find us to see who we were thinking they would ally with us; or some just wanted to ally with anyone.

Vince looked over at the pairs that had already crossed and smirked puffing out his chest as if to dare them to go against him.

But were any of these thoughts truthful? We couldn't tell.

We needed to move as others were coming so as we started towards the exit carefully and quietly, suddenly two guys appeared in front of us. We had our guns ready "Neat trick," they both said at once "What else can you do?" Again, at once. They looked a little older than us but not by much, maybe a year or two. They were the same, twins.

Katie pointed her gun and rushed at them; they disappeared, then reappeared behind us. I threw a rock right at them; it went right through them; they weren't there at all.

"It's an image," they both said again at the same time. They were clearly identical as we looked at them more clearly.

They were blond haired, piercing green eyes, good looking guys dressed in muddied jeans and runners, wearing hoodies with a few blood stains.

They looked like they had been through hell. What were they doing here? What did they want?

"Neat," Katie said, breaking me away from my thoughts. She raised her eyebrow at me and continued, "So, what else can you do or can both of you do?" she asked in a flirty way.

They both smiled at the same time "you'll see." They said, "Join us and find out, ally with us."

"Heads up," I said. "Almost there at the exit, be ready" Katie nodded.

The guys had disappeared, "what do you think? About the guys? Cute, right? Should we join them? They could be handy." Katie said with a smile.

I shrugged and rolled my eyes "Seriously at a time like this? I think we have bigger problems right now," I said.

When we got near the exit, there was already fighting going on. It looked like someone had beat us to the exit. This bald guy and tattooed lady were fighting together; she was shielding him while he was levitating boulders, crushing them, and throwing them at Vince and his buddy with no real effect.

Vince's buddy was laughing like this was so much fun. He threw knives at the lady, but they didn't get through her shields, so he began running at her shield with his body. Each time he did that, he was thrown back, but he kept going even as he was bleeding just laughing like he had nothing to lose. Meanwhile, Vince was hitting the boulders and cracking them. The guy looked at the lady, he nodded at her, and she seemed to do nothing, but the guy grabbed an even bigger boulder and threw it at Vince's friend. The rock shattered and the crazy guy fell, small rocks flew all over, but none hit them. She had expanded her shield to cover them both. Her partner began throwing the small rocks at Vince, it was like small knives hitting him and he fell to the ground, bleeding and having a hard time getting up. Her partner kept going throwing more rocks while he was down, not allowing him to get up at all.

I felt relieved it was over; they had won; Vince's buddy wasn't getting up and neither was Vince. The lady fell over exhausted, and he rushed to her. They won or so we thought but Vince's buddy suddenly stood, threw the rock to the side and shook himself off. "What a rush," he laughed. "How much time did I beat my record!?"

"Four minutes," Vincent said as he stood up bloodied but not defeated. "Shit, Mark, do a better job next time. You hardly dented the shield."

"My bad, too much fun, man. Plus, it worked, she's tired now and I doubt they'll be much fun anymore," Mark answered, "Let's finish them," he laughed.

"We need them; they could be useful to us." Katie said I nodded. I ran to the bald guy and lady; I nodded at them and helped them stand.

They looked surprised but nodded at me. "Now," I yelled, and Katie, she was there in an instant, both hands out Mark hit her shield hard and bounced back. She was levitating towards him; he seemed surprised but smiled. I grabbed her shoulder; she slammed her arms down hard and he hit the ground so hard we heard his bones breaking and he looked broken, he wasn't moving, he was done.

Vince looked at us with a grin "I knew you had more kitties," he said through his bloodied smile, he got up slowly, shook himself off looked at his partner and continued smiling he didn't seem to care he was down, he then rushed at us.

We grabbed the couple and ran as fast as we could, disappearing past them.

We had passed the exit just barely and joined the other teams that had crossed before us. The lady and tattooed guy thanked us and said we could align with them thought, honestly, I wondered about that.

I looked around quickly and noticed an older lady and older man, I'd say in their 50s, staring at us they hadn't moved at all. They had just watched everything go down, no reaction at all; they seemed to be looking for something. They were completely separated from the rest of the group, and they weren't even dirty like the rest of the groups there. I wondered when they had gotten there.

Vince was about to come after us, but the elder man raised his palm, and Vince stopped "They crossed the finish line," he said, "Leave them and keep looking; you can have the rest; we told you what we wanted so focus on that only and stay out there."

Vince looked angry but obeyed; he also looked a bit shaken when the man looked at him, like fright, maybe? I wasn't sure.

Who was this couple to shake him that way to even shut Vince up?

Mark got up, his broken limbs cracking and repairing. "Shit," he said and looked at Katie as he was standing up and cracking his bones and as they were fixing themselves, it was gross. He was finally done, and he smiled "I would love to play again, darling; that was fun," he smiled at Katie and blew her a kiss.

She shuddered. "Argh, disgusting," she said shaking herself off.

We were startled as we heard a laugh and saw the guys from before sitting beside us, the twins. They were covered in blood; it wasn't at all what we had seen them look like before. They noticed us staring "Not ours of course" they said to us in unison.

"It will be soon, you little shits," Vincent raged. "You got away last time but that won't happen again; you both got lucky, disappearing suddenly." He ran to them and grabbed one of them by their shirt. The one he grabbed put his hands up.

"Idiot" the elder lady said in an icy tone, "They already passed you; they were with the girls; couldn't you tell? Couldn't you feel they were with them this whole time?" she said, "Now get out there with your partner, idiot."

I jumped, and so did Katie. We hadn't noticed they were with us; we hadn't felt them at all. Vince forcefully threw the twin back and glared at him.

"I'll get you for what you both did," he said.

He went back to the exit; his buddy hadn't crossed yet, so he was able to go back out.

They were sitting next to us, one on each side. "Hi," they each smiled at us I couldn't tell them apart much like I had before "Are you..." Katie started to say. "Yes, twins," they smiled "We started off with you, but you must have forgotten us," the right twin said.

"You can project your images, right?" I spoke.

"Not quite right," one of them reached for my hand and passed right through me! I was shocked.

"Lisa, your mouth is wide open," Katie laughed. It was the first time we had at all smiled or yet alone laughed during this whole ordeal.

"Omg, I'm so sorry," I said, shyly smiling and looking down. We sat in silence for a bit, I was about to ask something else when I saw two more teams coming.

They seemed tired and drained; they looked really beat up "Get out of the way your big lug," one of the guys said looking around past Vince.

Vince smiled, "From where I'm standing, looks like you and your partner are on the way out." He chuckled.

"Oh, I'm okay just taking it easy" the guy leaning against his partner said and he chuckled a little. "There are many stronger groups still left and you trust me, we are stronger than you. Yes, we may be bit damaged, but we heal fast, and did you ever think we get this way cause we weak!

107

We get this way by killing others for fun." His eyes were blood red, he looked around at the other teams, smiling completely ignoring Vince.

He had a thick accent, Italian maybe or Romanian, I wasn't sure.

"Weak," he chuckled. "All you pass by as sneaky little bastards; none of you fought for your lives like we did; we take pleasure in our kills but all of you have not enough smell of blood on any of you; none are stronger or crave the fights like us. I can tell by looking at each of you that there's not enough bloodshed, not enough smell, mmmmmm, of blood that is so delicious and empowering," he said.

We instantly knew these guys were trouble and it was best to stay far away from them; they were probably one of the ones that were happy with what Jax had made us.

As he was talking, I noticed his wounds closing as well as his partner's wounds, yet his partner remained hunched over being held by his partner, as if he were in a lot of pain like his partner.

His eyes were blood red too, and he had a permanent grin on his face, like nothing bothered him, like he was just there to watch and take it all in.

Meanwhile, Vince was just blabbing away, saying he was stronger, just egging them on his partner Mark beside him smiling and moving around doing punches in the air as he continued to taunt them saying how they were going to die and how he and Mark were going to end them. He was laughing and puffing out his chest to intimidate the newcomers as Mark laughed and continued moving around.

I felt like my stomach dropped and I had a bad feeling I didn't like the guy, but I felt they were in danger, and it was going to end badly.

The two newcomers continued looking around and stopped staring at the older couple who were not looking their way uninterested by what was happening. These guys creeped me out and Katie grabbed my hand. She looked at me, and she seemed scared; I knew she felt the death around these two guys and the unease that I felt.

The way they looked around at all of us that had crossed already with such hunger in their eyes, it felt like they wanted to eat everyone there, it was scary. These guys were not to be messed with, and I was glad we never ran into them. It felt like they really enjoyed killing and hunting others.

All we could do was look to see what would happen next.

The guy holding his injured partner said, "I'm Lucius," his voice was soft and friendly, yet it felt menacing and threatening at the same time.

I'd thought I'd let you know before you die, my partner here is Julius; we love fights and kill many and damn, your teeth would be a nice addition to my collection." He said this as he grinned showing his razor-sharp teeth "I do love the taste of the kill." He spoke.

Katie gave a startled jump and squeezed my hand. I felt her fear; these guys were killers and they enjoyed it.

Vince jumped back suddenly as Mark stood beside him, excited. "Let's get em, get em good." He was smiling. "I'll wipe that grin off your stupid face, Lucy, was it?" Mark laughed.

"Yeah, enough talking, time to die," Vincent said.

"You're right, time to die," Lucius said calmly, letting go of his partner. He stood there for a moment, still with a grin on his face. He was handsome with jet black hair, a little built with some tattoos but he was also scary and intimidating at the same time.

I saw Mark's body fall and blood spattering everywhere, his head rolled, still smiling like he never felt anything or saw anything coming, and he never even got a chance to move.

"What the fuck!" Vince's surprise yell was loud heard by everyone.

Lucius laughed, "Oh, Julius, too fast, too fast, you take all the fun out of everything," he said.

"You know we need them scared; they taste so much better with a touch of fear, don't you think? Come on, let's play the game. You know I love the game."

"Fine," Julius said. He seemed a bit annoyed. He was beside Vince now and I hadn't even seen him move; he was so fast; he was dangerous for sure; they both were.

He touched Vince, then jumped back to join his partner "Ok, I'm sorry, Lucius but he was so annoying and couldn't be helped. His stupid smile, I just couldn't help myself" He looked at Vince, then said, "Choose a body part." He was looking at Vince and continued, "Go on now, what can you live without, what won't you miss as much once gone and Lucius will see if you are right."

"What the fuck," Vince said, and chuckled in surprise.

"Choose or I choose for you...." Julius grinned at Vince, who said nothing. "Ok, I'll take your tongue, I don't like hearing the noise coming out of you filled with nothing but stupidity."

"Oh no patience Julius, let him think, poor lug he already seems to have troubles thinking by himself, come on now" Lucius said.

Vincent gave a nervous laugh chest puffed out like he wasn't intimidated at all, but I saw him shaking a little. Suddenly, without warning, he was choking on his own blood, and he started screaming. A muffled scream came out. It was like a high-pitched wail and gurgling choking noise.

He held his hand over his bleeding mouth; he couldn't say anything and didn't have a chance to. He just held his hands over his mouth, the blood running down, all he could do was to try and hold himself together. He was shaking uncontrollably, and while watching him, we all felt a wave of pain that seemed to hit all of us in a forceful wave.

That's when I realized what his ability was, it was sending pain. He was able to send out his pain to anyone near; that was probably what had helped him to keep fighting, sending his pain away from himself to others so that he couldn't feel it himself, but it didn't seem to be helping him now.

I couldn't listen to him anymore, couldn't take the pain and was shaking from the pain waves being sent out, so I covered my ears and looked away trying to block his screams but still I felt the pain Katie put her head on my shoulder and whimpered. I looked around and noticed the others also shaking and shifting around with his pain; I looked over and saw a girl faint, it hurt so much this was unbelievable.

Julius stood there holding Vince tongue as if to show everyone his price. "Now what next are you choosing or am I?" he asked Vince who swung at him, missing completely, falling over.

"End it, know you fools," the lady with the older guy, who hadn't said anything till now, spoke forcefully her thick European accent coming through.

Julius and Lucius looked up at the pair and they suddenly bowed and stood still, looking at the ground as if they had just gotten into trouble. I don't know why or what had happened but in a red blur, Vince was dead. The waves of pain stopped releasing the hold on everyone.

I looked away, my eyes tearing up from the pain I had felt. This had been the guy that I'd been afraid of. This was the guy I hadn't wanted to face. I looked horrified at what I saw next the guy Julius he ripped open Vince's chest and ate at Vince's heart, and Lucius did the same to Mark and ate his heart. They crossed the exit and looked at the elder pair and bowed again.

"My dear lady, my sovereign, our apologies; we had no idea you and your husband were among us. Again, our apologies; if there is anything we can do, we will do it," he said and bowed again. His partner did the same. They looked over at her partner and did the same.

The elder guy nodded at them as if recognizing them for what they had just done. They took a seat near them, and the lady looked at them as if disgusted, but her partner whispered something, and she gave a quick smile to both and a quick nod.

They began speaking with her partner; he gestured something to them; they went over to the lady and had some words I couldn't hear; and Julius and Lucius both smiled. They went behind the lady and disappeared? They reappeared moments later, cleaned up, and well dressed in black suits.

They stood in front of the couple as if guarding them like bodyguards.

What had happened, and who were these people? I looked over at Katie, but she was watching the exit anxiously.

I was still shaking and felt Katie grab my hand, which calmed me down.

With all the excitement I hadn't even noticed that the twins had left us; they were now talking with Julius and Lucius, and they were let through to speak with the older couple; they all stood together but I couldn't hear anything once again. They were saying something and glanced our way and nodded as if discussing us, but I still couldn't hear anything they said. I wondered if this was one of their talents. It was like a shield around the couple; they nodded at the twins. The man placed his hand on one of their shoulders, and they too were gone.

We waited anxiously to see who would be the next to come.

End of part two.

# Light & Dark

# Prelude

"Is this it? The Portal?" I asked, looking at Ryan, his hazel eyes staring back at me.

He nodded. "Yes, Emily, this is it. Once we go through, they won't be able to track us. The baby will be born, and she will be the change that's needed. I can feel it. She will be the catalyst. She will change the world. "I love you," he said, squeezing my hand.

We stepped through the portal; it was dark, and I couldn't see anything in front of me. I held on to his hand. Had he really done it? Had we crossed to the middle ground? I saw Ryan wave his hand again; a shining light appeared above us to light our way. I held his hand tighter.

We had to make it the only way for our child to grow and be happy to live undetected. We knew this child wasn't supposed to be born and that we were never meant to have been together, but we fell in love and kept it secret. Then I got pregnant and now this child could throw everything off balance. The guardians would find us if we didn't escape.

"Em," Ryan said. "We're almost there to the Middle Ground. I have created a home away from everyone and everything. We can stay there forever, live there, and the balance wouldn't be shifted." He continued.

After darkness, there was light, and we were in a field. I saw that the house was beautiful, like I had always dreamed of having. Huge windows, a front porch, and my favorite color, purple, I fell in love right away. Inside was a white, open space where we could decorate as we wanted and where our child could grow up. There was a beautiful table and a baby highchair in the kitchen. The house was furnished and ready to move in.

I smiled. "I love it, Ry," I said. We had really done it; this was going to be the start of our new life away from magic and everything.

We lived blissfully with our little Emiry for a whole year. We were happy, and she was beautiful, but I noticed on her first birthday that she began showing signs of magic in her and I couldn't pinpoint it but whenever she got fussy, her strength was unimaginable her power. We couldn't hold it back it took our combined strength to keep things from flying around or catching fire. To just control it and calm her down. But when she was happy, beautiful flowers would blossom, butterflies would show up and there was a warmth that just made us happy as well.

She exhibited both of our powers, and I knew she was the catalyst, the one that could shift the balance and corrupt the balance. We had to stay here or else the guardians would find her and take her away or worse, kill her.

Ryan said he felt something coming and he felt it was no longer safe here. We needed to leave. I started packing but it was too late; they had found us.

The house was surrounded; both groups were there. The Guardians were in full force; they had found us. We stepped outside, hand in hand.

We knew how this was going to end but we needed to try. I pleaded with them to let her live so that we could watch after her and that her death wasn't the way, but our pleas weren't being heard. Both the Coven leaders were there, and our pleas went unanswered.

Some fired at us, the magic hitting our shields and cracking them then others came at our shield, pounding at it and rejecting their hits, but we weren't doing so great.

I looked around for Lousie, my best friend and my guardian since I was six. I saw her at the back; she was talking to someone I couldn't see.

I saw her pull out her enchanted blades, one Silver, the other Onyx, and come rushing into the battle. She pushed back some of the other guardians; they looked at her confused, some rushed at her, but she quickly did an enhancement chant and was not letting the others advance on her. She looked back at me, and I remembered she was always one of the strongest guardians, one of the most gifted, and my friend. The windows shattered behind us, and the house was coming down.

The guardians suddenly stopped; they looked over at Ryan and me.

Louise stepped in, and she nodded towards me to lower the shields I let go of Ryan and his shield dropped.

"What are you doing?" he said. "You know what they'll do; we have to fight."

Lousie said "Emily, we must bind the child, so she causes no danger, but you know what the sacrifice for doing that is. If you want her to live, this is the only way I will watch her but if no sacrifice is given for her to live, you all must perish. Let us bind her, please." She begged. .

"Ryan, she can't die; you know this; she's meant for so much more; I will make the sacrifice, please; we don't have much time." I spoke.

Ryan just stood there, his face ashen and he shook his head his eyes teared up.

"You know what that means, are you sure about this? You know that it may not be true that they just might be lying, and we all die, Em, please. "He begged holding my hand. "Em, please, I can make the sacrifice; it doesn't have to be you, plus we don't know yet what she will be or if she will be. You know the bindings can take all her power away and then she can be just normal, nothing more. Or you can all just leave us here and we won't set foot in your world again, please don't do this" he said.

"You know this can't be guaranteed; she will grow and get curious, and she will come home and the shift in balance will be broken. We don't know what she is; we can't take the risk; it's better for her to disappear." The leader of white spoke.

I saw Ryan look furious at his father, the Coven Leader for Light.

"I'm ready, Ryan I know what I must do; she needs to live please take care of her," I said.

"Louise Please take care of her she; balances everything currently and Ryan, don't lose heart. I know it will be hard, but you can do it, you can be there for her. I love you. Stay with our child." I spoke looking at Ryan please as tears began running down my face.

The chanting started Louise hugged me "I promise I will watch her as if she were my own; she will grow up away from everything until it's time for her choosing." She spoke.

"I can't do this without you, my love." Ryan pleaded, holding my hand.

The chanting grew louder, and I felt a dagger pierce my heart. Louise held the dagger as I faded, and I saw tears streaming down her face.

# Light & Dark

I woke up shaking, with cold sweat running down my back and I felt clammy.

Same dream again I can't remember most pieces of it they are, like broken parts.

The part I remember most is walking through an empty house, the sun shining, tattered curtains, broken windows, dust everywhere, broken dishes, and burn marks on pieces of what had been a house. It was like an explosion happened from the inside, bursting outwards. The walls were stained with burn marks, part of the roof was missing, and the furniture knocked over was all burned or scorched. I walked through the house towards an old armchair with burns and the cushions ripped, and there were books. There's someone there and as I get closer, I wake up. The dream ends.

Lately, I've been seeing more of the house as I walk through it; a burned teddy bear on the ground, a small table with rotten food on it, two shattered plates on an oak table lightly burned and the weather. It feels warm like it's summertime. I get closer to the old armchair and that's where I usually wake up, but I feel like this location is real, that it's calling to me, that my dreams aren't dreams but reality and that they are leading me somewhere and I need to find out where.

I couldn't see anything that could help me get to the house, just an open field and darkness. I kept dreaming about that.

I've been dreaming about that place for the last six months. There was nothing familiar, no signs. The sun shone on the torn down house but when I looked out, everything else was pitch black. I had absolutely no clue where this place was, but I felt no, I knew that I had to get there because it was real. Something was stirring in me. I felt energy within me, and it felt strange and foreign.

"Emiry, Are You Up?" Louise called.

"Yes, I'll be down soon," I called back, lying on my bed still. I got up and changed quickly.

This dream kept haunting me, and it seemed to be taking over my thoughts. I sometimes saw images of the house when I was awake. I decided to tell Louise because we had always made a promise to tell each other if things were bothering us. I wanted to see if she had any opinions on what this constant dream could mean.

I told her, and she just said dreams are parts of everything that happened throughout the day, week, months, some memories, movies, things like that. Some had no real meaning, and she just brushed it off, but I noticed that she seemed a bit nervous when I told her about the house I saw. I waited to see if she would say anything at all she cleared her throat and she then changed the subject as usual when she didn't seem to want to continue discussing things she didn't want to, so I decided to drop it.

Louise Fletcher had been my mother's best friend since they were young; she had raised me after my mother had passed away. She had told me they had been friends since they were young, and she always told me what she remembered about her, her smile, and that she had been kind, so that I knew a bit about my mother, she told be funny stories and how much they had supported each other, I loved those stories.

She never felt like a mother, more like a friend or older sister. I had a few pictures of my mother and Louise's stories about her helped me imagine what she may have been like but other than that I had nothing else.

She had always said my mother had left me something special for me and when it was time, I'd inherit it. As for my father, she said he had never been around and that she didn't know him well enough to say much about him, but she said they met in high school and when I asked Louise if she remembered more about him, she said no and that he had left us then changed the subject like always.

To me, my father was a mystery. I didn't know anything about him other than the rare things Louise had said, she never liked to talk about him. She did say my parents had met in school, where they all attended; she said he was never around after I had been born.

His family moved away, and they had never reached out to us and as for my mother's parents, they had never kept in touch after my mother had passed and they had given custody rights to L so I figured we were better off since it seemed my so called family on both sides didn't care or had tried to get to know me.

I sometimes wondered about my father, why he had left or tried harder, if he had a new family and if he ever thought about me. I really knew nothing about him Louise refused to speak much about him, she sometimes seemed angry when I asked so I just figured he was a deadbeat and I that we were better off without him, and I had never received anything from him, and I never really asked much about him.

My childhood had been happy and normal, just me and L against the world we didn't need anyone else we were happy and yes sometimes it had been rough but L always put me first, I wondered if she sometimes regretted taking me in but she never gave me any clues she ever regretted me and she always said I was the best part of my mother and it felt like she lived through me so she said it was like her friend was still around.

She never really talked about her parents; they had passed when she was young, and she was an only child, but she did have a few distant relatives. We had met one of her cousins when I was like five but yeah, she didn't keep in touch with them much and honestly, she was all I really needed; she was my family.

"Hey Em, please don't forget breakfast; at least a pop tart, please." Louise said to me.

From the door, I saw her putting her shoes on as I made my way down the stairs. I noticed on her hand there was a new ring on her left ring finger and three small symbols; a half-moon, a shooting star, and a circle with something in it I noticed the one in the middle looked cracked.

"Hey, cool ring," I said, pointing at her hand.

She grabbed her car keys and put her hand in her pocket fast "Ummm, thanks, it's not really my style but a friend from work gave it to me and you know just felt.... ummmm, shoot, look at the time I got to go, bye Hun," she said and rushed out the door.

I put my hand up, waved bye, headed to the kitchen, grabbed some pop tarts, put them in the toaster, grabbed a glass of orange juice and drank it quickly.

I began getting my bag ready. It was the last day of classes, and I was officially done with school and exams. I then would head to university to be a microbiologist or, well, anything I wanted, or so I thought. I never expected how quickly things would change.

When I got home, Louise was home too; she was in the kitchen getting dinner ready.

"Hey, kiddo, listen. I want to talk to you about your birthday tomorrow, a big day, you'll be eighteen. There're a few things you need to know, ok?"

"Yup, I know. Big changes: University just around the corner, it will be insane, I can't wait," I called excited thinking about my future as I headed to my room.

Louise said something else, not sure what I couldn't hear since I had my headphones back on, but I felt like something brushed against my skin. I turned around; nothing was there. "Weird," I said out loud and I headed to my room.

When I got back downstairs, Louise was setting the table, and she sat next to me like usual.

"It's extremely important that you come straight home tomorrow. I have a surprise for you, so no strangling. Okay, tomorrow, come straight home," she said.

This stopped me from eating. I looked up at her with a smile. "Yeah, a surprise. Can I get any clues?" I looked at her again with a smile on my face, but she seemed serious, not her usual self. This felt different so I stopped smiling.

"Why can't you tell me now?" I asked.

"Just please come straight home tomorrow, ok? There're a few things we need to go over about your parents," she answered in a serious tone, then changed the subject to her usual avoidance tactic.

"Sure," I said, picking at my plate. I knew a bit about my mother, but she never really said anything about my father, and she had mentioned parents, which was strange. She finished and left the room before I could say anything.

"Night, I have an early day tomorrow, so I'll probably be gone before you wake up. Straight home okay." I heard her yell from the hallway.

I couldn't sleep that night. I kept having the dream of that empty house with the tattered interior but there was more. I saw overturned furniture and began walking towards the room with burnt books on the floor, and I saw someone sitting on the chair this time. I didn't wake up this time. I walked up to the chair; I saw a man sitting there. I noticed a silver ring on his finger. he was holding a book with a silver cover and the same symbols looked like Louise's ring but slightly different, more complete, not broken, it looked like shooting star pieces scattering.

I moved around to see him but what he said froze me in place I couldn't move "Emiry, today is the day you'll decide, there's nothing more important than this, you must choose correctly. I'm sorry, I wasn't there for you. I couldn't be there; we had no idea," he said sounding a little sad.

I woke up, just shaking, and cold sweat ran down my back. Who was that!? He seemed familiar but I couldn't see his face. But I felt like I knew him, I felt drawn to him.

Louise didn't call me down that day; it felt strange, but I knew she had left early for work. I washed up and got ready for the last day of school.

I went downstairs and saw a note on the table, folded and wax sealed. The paper felt old, it looked stained, and the seal had the same symbol as the book. I opened the note.

*Emiry,*

*Happiest of Birthdays today, my darling, Emiry. Know that no matter what, these years with you were the greatest. I was able to see the strong woman you've become, and I do cherish you my little star.*

*Nick will be here to pick you up, I'm sorry I won't meet you like I said I would. I'll leave a bag packed for you. Please remember, come straight home, this is very important!*

*Love,*
*L.*

Nothing else was written but I noticed on the bottom of the note, there were the symbols again but this time it was a half-moon then a full moon with shooting stars scattering. I touched the paper, and the symbols were raised. I touched the symbols again; they felt hot, then cool like ice...weird.

It was unusual for Louise to use fancy paper for a note and not say anything else; it was all so cryptic but exciting. Maybe we were going on a fancy trip she had planned for us; she always said when I turned eighteen it was going to be special.

I headed to school excited about my trip. We had a last school ceremony for us seniors, homeroom check-in then handing in our books, clearing the desks and just telling stories of our high school experiences. Then, at lunch, seniors all sat together laughing and having fun. It was nice. By the time the last period came, we were cleaning out our lockers no class. I sighed. This was it; I wasn't going to be coming back here, I looked around and smiled I had an amazing high school experience no bad memories I could think of all that had happened prepared me for all that was going to come.

"Emiry!" My friend ran over and gave me a huge hug. "Hey Ella," I hugged her back.

"We are all heading to Don's; are you coming to the last hoorah?" she asked excitedly.

"I can't; I'm apparently heading on a trip and can't be late Louise's friend Nick is picking me up from our place." I smile a little.

"Oh, hot Nick, nice, well, okay then... omg, you haven't signed my yearbook, oh, and none of that. Keep in touch, have a great summer junk," she laughed as she handed me her yearbook and a pen.

I wrote, "Thanks for sticking by me and always making me smile and laugh even when I didn't think I could. I'll see you at Uni, but we will get together before then." I drew a heart and a winky face and signed my name as I handed her the book. I also noticed I had drawn the moon and shooting stars.

"When?" I said it out loud without meaning to say it.

"When What?" Ella said.

"Nothing, forget it." I gave her a hug.

"I'll see you after we get back; I got to go. I'll text you later and send some pics from my mystery trip" I smiled and gave her another hug, saying goodbye, and headed home quickly, unaware that so much was about to change.

Nick came to get me around 4 p.m. He was tall, sandy blonde hair, well-built and had green piercing eyes. He was very handsome, if only I was older, I thought.

"Hey kid, ready to go?" He spoke.

Well, that was a blow, I sighed and nodded. He thought of me as just a kid still, and why not. What was I expecting him to see me differently somehow?

"Yup, ready," I said.

We got in his truck and just kept driving for a couple of hours. I asked where we were going but he said he'd never driven there before and that Louise had given him directions on his GPS, and he was just following them, but I felt like he was lying.

We arrived at a beautiful home located in the middle of nowhere in a wooded area; it was like an old-style mansion. The mansion was beautiful light yellow with four large columns holding up a large balcony, the front porch, and a sitting area.

"Wow," I said as I got out of the car.

Louise came outside dressed in a beautiful red satin gown, an onyx necklace around her neck, and a matching ring with the symbols inside the Jem I had seen the inside looked like was moving inside the ring, but the ring was different than before. The star was in the circle of the full moon, and she also wore the same on her right ring finger.

She thanked Nick for getting me here. We unloaded the bags, and she hugged Nick. She seemed to whisper something to him, and he nodded, looked at me, and said bye.

A maid came out and took my bags. "Miss Marlowe, it's an honor to meet you," she said.

"My name's not Marlowe; it's Emiry Castles," I replied.

"Yes, miss," she said with a quick bow and took my bag.

"What is this, Louise?" I asked, surprised and excited. "This is wow. What in the world is all this? Who does she think I am? Also, look at you, you look amazing. Is this some sort of extravagant party you forgot to tell me about? Are we secret millionaires?" I smiled. I continued asking questions "Who do you know who has this crazy money? Did you save up all these years for this? Wow you've outdone yourself," I said, excited.

Louise took a deep breath "It will all be explained to you soon. Now, come, I'll show you to your room you need to wash up and get ready. I'll be waiting to help you get ready once you're done washing up, okay?" she said.

I nodded slowly and said "Ready for what? Seriously, why are you dressed up? Not that you look bad, but wow, never did I think I'd see you like this and what is happening?" I asked her.

She didn't answer as I followed her up the stairs.

This all caught me off guard; she looked so beautiful, and she had never been like this, not in all the years we had lived together.

Now, what was all this to help me get ready? She had only ever done that when I was small but that had stopped after I turned ten. She then became more like a friend or an older sister.

We entered a large, beautiful room. There was a black laced Tulle Dress with a corset bustier, the dress was long and flowing. It was embroidered with gold stars, full moons, and half-moons. It was beautiful. I've never seen anything like this before; a trial of stars on the bottom of the dress. All I could think was, wow, how much was this gown and the shoes beside it?

"What the hell was this?" into the room looking around.

I took a shower and came out smelling fabulous. I felt like I had just walked into a fairy tale; there was a maid in the room waiting for me. She was placing some beautiful jewelry on the vanity. I felt like I was in an expensive hotel that we could never afford in a million years, but I also felt a sense of fear and panic that something was about to happen and that I shouldn't be here at all.

There was a knock on the door and the maid answered it. As I stood there in the bathrobe, I felt so out of place.

The maid opened the door Louise stepped through, and she dismissed her; we were left alone now, just me & her.

I looked at her and she was dressed in another beautiful black gown fading to blue at the bottom; it was flowing, and a long, delicate silver necklace decorated her neck with a small blue sapphire.

I sat down on the Vanity I picked up a silver hairbrush; it was heavy and beautiful, and it had a moon on the handle.

Louise came up behind me, extended her hand palm out, and I gave her the brush. She had a small silver box; and she set it down beside me and began brushing my hair, while I looked down. It reminded me of when I was younger and all the laughs we had and stories she would tell me about her day.

I looked at the small box of silver with the same type of symbol I had seen all throughout the day. "I need to know what's going on, L. please tell me, this house, the clothes, what's going on?" I asked.

Louise took a deep breath "This is your house, and everything in it is yours to inherit. After tonight, you're going to meet your real family, they are from your father's side and your mother's. You'll be asked to choose what you'll be and who you'll be. Everything will change after tonight." She spoke.

She continued "Truthfully, this is a ceremony a sort-of graduation for you to see if you possess magic and what type. Also, to see if you have any magic ability in you and that will tell them which type of magic you possess and whichever type you'll inherit."

I sat there quietly; I had no words and no idea what to say. What was she talking about? Magic? That wasn't real and what was this whole inheritance thing about? I was so confused.

She continued, "Both your parents were extremely powerful, one light and one dark, and each possessed unique skills of their own, they were exceptional they were born to be the next leaders. They should never have been together, but they were, and then came you, which, threw everything off balance. So, when you were born, this caused quite a stir in both their families, but your parents really loved each other and were happy so they ran away. They hid you from everyone; your father created a portal and lived there with you until they were found. The place you see in your dreams is real but it's in another reality." She looked at me while still brushing and fixing my hair.

She continued "The house you dream of is where you all lived, hidden away from everything, from here, from this world, by your parents. I'll tell you this world isn't for everyone the magic world is not all that seems. The realm the one you were hidden in it is chaotic and full of strong magic; it's unruly and dangerous, but you survived, which means you're strong even though you haven't yet chosen." She went silent as she noticed I was so silent.

"I'm sorry, Emiry. I promised your mother I'd hide from you this world, but as you grew, they sensed you, and when you turned eighteen, you became or had the potential to be the catalyst, and everyone sensed it. I promised not to tell you anything, as I was trying to protect you. I wanted you to have a normal life. I hoped you would have a normal life but now I just don't know." She spoke as she continued brushing my hair.

"How..." I looked in the mirror at my hair it was up in a bun but still flowing down, my hair which had always been a dark purple since I was little looked beautiful; there was a beautiful blue Sapphire star pin in the bun. I hadn't felt her doing anything, as I had been too consumed by my thoughts.

"Hey, I got you something," Louise said.

She gave me the silver box and I opened it. Inside was a necklace with crashing stars the scattered pieces were onyx diamonds that decorated the chain; it was so beautiful.

"It was your mother's; she wore it for her ceremony. When she was to become the next leader of Dark, she was already powerful without the gifts she gained but she became much, much more," she said.

She met your father shortly after that, as there have always been disagreements with light and dark magic. What seems good may not always be good, but none the less, they fell in love at first sight, according to your mom." She smiled and continued. "But she knew that there always needed to be a balance, so this wasn't allowed; they kept their love secret. I knew about their love, but she was my best friend, and I just couldn't break her heart so I kept their secret." She looked down with a sad expression on her face.

"How, how could you not tell me all this about my parents and my nightmares? What am I or what can I become? " I found myself shaken by this person I'd known all my life, the one who had always avoided my questions and then this, just this whole thing—what the hell, how could she keep this from me? She had always been my best friend as well, and now I knew she had been my mother's best friend as well.

"What or who are you?" I composed myself and it just burst out suddenly without me thinking of how I would make her feel.

"I'm" she paused. "I'm your guardian, I have been trained to fight and have abilities that are mainly defensive and restraining abilities that assist in blocking other magical abilities that may be a danger to others and others like me. We use these abilities to guard the balance of the world. I've kept you safe until the time arrived for your choosing. As I said, I'm part of several families around the world. We are the guards, the ones that help keep the balance in the world, the peace between Light and Dark, and if that balance falls, we help restore the balance. We track those who are not following the rules of our world." She looked over at me to see if I had any questions about what she had just revealed.

I cleared my throat and asked "By doing what exactly? What do you do to restore this balance?" My voice cracked, afraid of what she might say.

She paused, then continued, "You'll learn more about my family and yours. I'm sorry I couldn't tell you, but it was for your own good. I never meant to hurt you in any way I hope you'll forgive me," she said, putting the necklace on me and resting her hands on my shoulders.

I placed my hand where hers was. "I do forgive you, how could I not. I love you. But I'm hurt that you never prepared me for any of this, you're the only family I've ever known. I'm hurt. These was a big secret you've kept from me, but you said you were also doing it for my protection, but I still don't know what you're protecting me from. Now I'm here and I don't know what to think. And all I can think of is that you're the only family I've ever known, and I think I'll need you more than ever. I don't seem to have a good feeling about this and well, it's weird I have this whole new amazing thing that you told me about but yet I don't have a good feeling and I wish well; why can't we just leave? I will forgive you and because you are my family and because my mother trusted, I have never had any doubts about you even now so of course will forgive you."

I got up and hugged her; it felt automatic what I did next and went over to the bed, picked up the dress and put it on. L helped button the back and tie the corset; it was a perfect fit.

"I just wish you could have told me earlier. I feel so lost right now and, in some ways, like I don't know you at all. These is so confusing to me, and I need you L you know and that well that I do love you so much I honestly don't understand what's going on and I know that I will need you with this whole thing." I spoke taking a deep breath as I looked down on the vanity and fiddled with the box.

"You know you remind me of Emily your mother," she said placing her hand in mine. I couldn't tell you and thank you for forgiving Me." she hugged me. "I will tell you this know that I'm your guardian, as I always have been, and that today you will have to choose light or dark, but I believe that you may be the catalyst possessing both types of magic and this is what I think you are and if you are well, things will get well, they will get difficult. I knew that you did need an environment away from the influences of all casters and this is what I did, and I kept you away as long as I could. But listen, I'm not supposed to tell you, but you can go back to the normal life you've always had. If you deny both your heritages, in doing that, you'll be stripped of all magic within you and your memories taken away. You can go back to being a normal kid, go off to school and just live out your normal life or you can choose and in doing so, you could throw off the balance, but you will also be able to learn about your heritage and maybe see your father again. But you can also be the Catalyst and with that comes great turmoil for both sides and a war might break out because you don't choose; you'll be controlling a large amount of power." She spoke.

My mother's name was Emily. I looked at myself, I didn't recognize this person looking back. I spoke "Why do you always say my father but not my mother, did something happen to her?" I asked but I feared I already knew the answer.

"What is my real name? Is it Marlowe? Not Emiry? I asked.

"It's Emiry Marlowe, not Emiry Castles," she said.

"Your name was changed to keep you hidden from those who believe you will bring chaos to our world but now it's time to be part of the world, our world, but again, you have a choice." she said, and began to lead me downstairs to the cellars of the mansion. I heard talking as there were others there.

"What will happen if I don't choose?" I asked.

"I told you that you can go back to your normal life. However, I won't be there. A new guardian will be placed, and new memories will be made so that you won't know the difference between what happened." She spoke sadly.

We stopped at two large wooden doors, the symbols all around them were shifting, but not moving they were all around the doors.

"I can't forget you, L. you've always been there. How can you just ask me to let you go? We are family, remember? That's what you've always said." I looked at her, my eyes beginning to tear up.

She squeezed my hand "Okay, get ready," Louise said and gave my hand another squeeze.

We stepped through the doors.

I looked around. It was like stepping into another world. I saw floating lights and the air felt warm. There were flower petals floating around us; it smelled like summer and a tree was at the center with pink petals and moving branches as if it were alive.

I walked slowly, just starting in amazement. Everything was so beautiful. I noticed a group of people, some in beautiful white cloaks, others in black cloaks, just as beautiful. They were each gathered on opposite sides of each other.

I looked at the center again; a beautiful woman in a beautiful black gown and black cloak and a flowing gown that looked like was moving gently in the breeze and a handsome man dressed in a white suite and white cloak were at the center now, each holding a glowing object, but I couldn't see what they held.

Louise stepped behind the Lady in black and I was surprised to see Nick was there too, dressed in a suit of similar color but not quite to match Louise, he had a white suit fading into blue at the ends of his sleeves and pants, and he had a sapphire ring. I realized he must be like L, a guardian, and that he had known all along what was going to happen that they both had known.

I felt a sense of panic as I got nearer to the tree where they both stood; my energy felt different.

I stood in the middle of the man; he looked at me and smiled warmly, which eased my fears, but the woman was not looking up at me as I neared them.

The woman spoke, "Emiry Marlowe, you are here to choose and also to see if you are the Catalyst that was never supposed to exist." She said this without a hint of emotion.

The man spoke, "Your existence brings great fear to both our ways of life, an unbalance to both our houses, and an unpredictable consequence to actions that should have never happened." He sounded almost sad.

I looked up at both of them and said, "I never knew my parents or this world you speak of; I don't know anything about the balance, magic, or what I may or may not become; if I have to choose, then I will, and if I make the wrong choice, all I ask is to meet my parents at least once, to know where I came from before....before you do anything or what you think you need to do." I spoke with a quiver of fear in my voice.

The lady finally looked at me, she looked as if she were trying to maintain her composure, then she spoke. I could feel her words like ice. "My daughter paid for the consequences for your existence, I will not have our houses unbalance again because of you. This is why all this is now happening, why the fear, and why we don't throw off the balance. This doesn't just affect you; it effects the world."

The man looked at me with soft eyes and said, "If you are the Catalyst, which I believe you are, there are great consequences to your existence and because you're part of both our houses, others may try to begin war, saying that we have thrown off the balance and they will retaliate and might also try to do the same as your parents did. We can't have that, you see; balance has always existed for over a millennium and the power has always been equally shared but with you for the first time in centuries, we don't have a clue what is next."

"Are you...my grandfather?" I asked, my voice shaking.

"Yes, I am your grandfather, and your father is my son. He ran away, you see; we haven't been able to track him, and I hope that now he will come back because of you because he knows you will need him and that you are safe. Know that I will try to always protect my family." He sounded sad.

I looked at the lady, who was still not looking directly at me; she was still avoiding my glance.

"Let's hurry up while the moon is high; I want this done, Now," she sternly said.

They placed their objects in the center of a floating stand.

I looked at the other people that were there who hadn't looked up as I had chatted with my grandparents. I had no clue what to do so I looked down at the objects that were still glowing, and they both began to float towards me. I heard a gasp from someone in the room as I reached towards both objects.

I held them both and I felt a rush of heat throughout my whole body, and it lifted me to the air. It was warm, then it got hot, then I screamed. I felt like I was boiling alive. I couldn't stop screaming. Then I heard chanting over my screams, then an immense bright light.

When I woke, L was talking to my grandmother, who kept pointing at me and raising her arms. She seemed really upset, and L kept putting her hand on her shoulder and my grandmother brushed it off and stormed off.

What had happened, I wondered? I looked down and saw I was still wearing the beautiful dress. My palms hurting, I looked at my palms one had a start then the other a moon shape it then fades. I started to remember what had happened, the light had been so bright and the chanting so loud and I don't remember the rest, but I knew it was bad I got scared, what was I now?

L came into the room I was in she stood at the doorway, "Hi," she said, "How are you doing, how are you feeling?"

"I think I'm okay" I paused "She hates me, doesn't she?" I spoke, looking at the door. "What happened? Where am I and what am I?" I asked.

She came to my bed and sat beside me. "I have something to tell you, love." She held my hand she sounded sad "I'm so sorry, but you are the Catalyst what they have feared you were and right now, there is discussion going on about what to do with you or how to deal with you. You see, your Grandparents, they are the heads of their covens and right now, your grandmother is upset; she doesn't know what to do. She doesn't know you like I do and she's having a hard time with this, and well, she isn't the easiest person to come around, but your grandfather he says he will take you in, and he wants to, ummm… he wants to train you. He says you've been gone too long, and you should have grown up in a proper house with family. Don't worry, I know things are changing fast and you're confused, but Nick will be there he knows you and you can trust him." She spoke.

"What about you? Will you be coming with me?" My eyes teared up and my voice quivered.

"No," she said, "I'm bound to your grandmother and her family and coven. I'm sorry, Emiry. I honestly thought you'd be able to, I thought you'd be able to make a choice to not be…." She stopped. "Emiry, your grandfather's house is different than what you're accustomed to. There are many rules as there are with both houses and all covens, but you won't have the freedom you're used to; you won't be able to come and go as you please. "Emiry" her voice quivered. "You won't be able to go away to university anymore; this life has been chosen for you. I'm so sorry, oh my dear Emiry if things were different if only…" She stopped and continued "Their coven, they are different; it's not all what you may be thinking."

"Why can't I stay here with you? Also, what do you think is different? What are you talking about?" I sat up on the bed even more confused than before. "The man seemed nice and kind." I spoke.

"You must rest, Emiry. A lot has happened and a lot more is to come. We will be at the estate for a few more days to help with your transition. Emiry, I do love you always, remember that, and I will always try checking in on you." Louise got up, gave me a hug, and left the room.

I sat awake for a long time just going through everything that had happened today; I didn't feel myself drifting off.

Suddenly I was back in that house; that burnt down house, I walked around, and I saw someone else there. He was standing there in jeans and a white t-shirt; his bronzed muscled skin showing through his shirt and his face was clean shaven and handsome; he had brown curly hair and hazel eyes; and his hands were in his pocket.

"Who are you?" I asked but, in a way, I already knew.

"My name is Ryan Marlowe, I sensed you when your power was released; your bind was broken. The one, I helped place in you with your mother, the only woman that I loved she was the love of my life." His hazel eyes stared at me he looked sad.

I took a deep breath. "Where have you been?" I asked.

"Emiry, I'm sorry, but you must listen. You can't go to my father's house; he will use you to start a war with the other covens. This is what he's been waiting for to find you to see if you possessed both magics. He isn't to be trusted. I know I haven't been there, but you don't deserve this. You were a product of Emily's and my love, and I know she wouldn't have wanted any of our families to have you. I'm in the middle ground, come to me, you'll be safe there," he said.

"Why should I trust you?" I responded.

"I've always loved you, even though it may not seem like I was there, I was watching over you when I could. Emiry, you must go to the middle ground; they won't be able to touch you here because it will be your decision and they can't get you. The reason they came for your mother and me was because we were throwing off the balance, but you have both of our essences in you, which means you're a more powerful weapon out there. They won't consider you anything but that. Please come to Middle ground I will be with you. I will help you. Control your power, please, trust me. I'll tell you what happened to your mother, I'll tell you everything I should have had before, and I'll tell you why I had to leave. Please, you can find me, and I will keep you safe."

I looked around the room and I had no idea what to say.

"You'll be waking up soon. Tell no one about our conversation and don't go with my father. As for your grandmother, I believe she is also unpredictable so it's best you find me soon. I'll explain everything to you what you are and what you can be. I know you don't trust me but trust yourself and think of me. It may take time, but I will be here waiting. I'll contact you again." He spoke.

"Honestly," I was about to say when a loud knock at the door woke me. Louise and my grandmother walked in.

"Hello Emiry, I am the leader of the House of Dark; my name is Eva Castles; my daughter was Emily Castles." She still wouldn't look at me. "She was your mother. I have always known that you existed," she looked at L and continued, "But I had chosen not to interfere, as it seemed best at that time." She spoke.

"What happened to her? I asked, my voice shaky.

"An unfortunate circumstance that could not be avoided," she said.

I heard her voice quiver a little, like she was holding back from crying.

"What unfortunate circumstance?" I asked.

She continued and avoided my question "I'm your grandmother and you are my granddaughter but you're also a danger to both our covens. In your choosing, you choose both Light and Dark, and that was not supposed to happen. Your choosing was supposed to be only one choice but now that you have both our powers, you are a Catalyst, a weapon, an unpredictable weapon at that, if swayed the wrong way, you could cause great harm not just to us but to others that aren't like us. We are two of the most powerful covens, we need to make sure you can control the power you seem to hold. I will train you myself if you want. Your choice, but just know that I don't want a war. I never have, but if you go with Light, there will be a war and there will be casualties, not just us but regular people that have nothing to do with this and know nothing of what we are. I have strong suspicions that Light will begin a war. We are look I would rather not have anything happen." She spoke.

"Why didn't you want to talk to me before? When I was at that choosing, you never even looked at me." I said, a bit hurt and angry.

"You remind me too much of Emily, of how she was at your age before she...before she was lost to me." She answered.

"I need to know more about her and why you never once contacted me if you knew I was alive. I need to know what you meant about the circumstances." I spoke.

"That is a long story, all you need to know right now is don't take Lights offer; they aren't what they seem, and they don't have your best interest," she said.

"But you do; you have my best interest, do you? My anger began to rise, and I noticed things began to rise in the air. I couldn't control it.

"Calm down," Louise said as she began moving slowly towards me and continued telling me to calm down.

I felt energy coursing through my body; it felt as if it wasn't mine, it wasn't me. I felt so much energy coursing through me that it felt burning hot, it lifted me off the ground. I saw things flying around the room and I could hardly focus on calming down. I could hardly hear Louise's voice. My whole body felt burning hot.

I looked over at my grandmother, who had her arms raised. She seemed to be saying something. I couldn't hear what she was saying. I saw L trying to come closer, but she was being pushed back by something I couldn't see but I saw a blade in her hand it shone, and I wasn't sure what I saw but she changed suddenly and wasn't wearing her dress anymore. She kept saying something I couldn't hear and was making gestures with her hands.

There was a strong wind surrounding me and pushing her back. She was saying something I couldn't hear, and she began slicing at the air and every time she sliced the air, she got closer to me.

"Emiry!" Louise yelled at me, "Calm down! You need to calm down, you're just showing what everyone is afraid of. Please this isn't you calm down!" She yelled.

I looked at my grandmother again, her arms still lifted.

"Now!" Louise yelled.

I was thrown on the bed and couldn't move; all I felt was my energy being drained and I felt so tired.

"I can't take much more; hurry," my grandmother winced in pain.

Louise moved so fast that she then sat beside me, "Emiry, please calm down. I understand the events today have been insane, but you must focus now on my voice. Please, calm yourself. Do you remember when you were ten, you remember how we used to count down from ten. Take a deep breath. Think of happy thoughts, and for one, the place you wanted to go to the most, where we said we would travel. Do you remember?" she asked while running her hand through my hair. "Do you remember when I said I'd always keep you safe? That hasn't changed. I want what's best for you, I always have." She continued. She touched my palm. I felt as if she was tracing a symbol on it the way she was touching it.

I burst into tears "I'm sorry, L, I'm so sorry, I just want to go home," I cried.

Louise turned to my grandmother, who still held her arms up and nodded. I saw her fall to her knees and take a deep breath. She seemed exhausted and tired.

I felt calmer and felt that I was able to move again. I looked at L, and she hugged me, and I hugged her back, crying. What is going to happen to me? I asked.

We heard a knock at the door. "Ma'am," a maid said. "The Lights are making arrangements and Lord Marlowe wants to speak with you," she said as she looked around the room, shocked.

"Thank you; tell him I will speak with him shortly." She replied as she got up.

She looked over at me and got up, her hair out of place and shuffled. She ran her hand on her hair and on her clothes and she was like she had been like nothing had happened.

"I will see if we can work out a deal where you can also stay with me and train since you have both Light and Dark in you. You'll need to learn both our ways; I will be back," she said.

I looked at L, "What is Middle Ground?" I asked.

She held my hand "Where did you hear that? You can't speak about that; who told you? Listen, Em, you can't let anyone know that you are aware of that place." she spoke.

"Do you understand? Come, let's get you ready," she said.

Ready for what exactly? I had already gone through so much that I didn't know if I could handle it anymore but I followed L as she left the room.


End of Part 1

# Finding A Home

# Why I Wrote "Finding A Home"

This story is not like my previous stories. It's different from the rest, as it has a lighter tone and I know it may seem like doesn't fit with the rest of what I have written but I hope it's enjoyed by whomever is reading. I wanted to add this story as it's important to me. It's dedicated to my Dogs who are a large part of me and who I am.

Yen & Sally

Jack

I had a wonderful dog named Jack who completely changed my life. He was silly, stubborn and always brought tons of laughs and joy to me and our family. After he passed away it was the hardest time but remembering him always brings a smile to my face dogs I believe are the most loyal and they are all unique in their own ways, Jack will forever be a part of me.

I want to believe that each of us can do our part to help animals in need and I also would like to believe Jack was as happy and had a wonderful life while he was with us.

I'm a huge animal lover and always have been. I always try to donate to organizations that help animals in need when I can.

I now have two rescues currently and they are amazing. They make me smile and I learn from them as they learn from me every day, each with their own unique attitudes.

One of them was my inspiration for this story, as the shelter she came from told us she was a street dog before being rescued by them. I hope, as you read, you decide to look into helping these societies if you don't already. Please support your local Rescue shelters and Animal Rescue Societies. Thank you for reading.

# Finding a Home

To me, this was my life survival at all costs: never stay in one place too long but move forward if you want to survive.

We were born in a small pack under a shelter away from the wetness, lights, and the noise. Mother cared for us as best she could; she brought back the little she'd been able to find and fed us all. Sometimes, I would notice she didn't join us to eat, but we drank the milk she provided us.

Mother focused on us, making sure we survived and learned as much as we could from her. With the time we had with her, we all felt loved.

We lost some of my siblings as we grew. We got curious and began wondering more on our own than as a pack like we had with mother, but we kept close. Some of my siblings were lost in the streets as not all of us were strong. Mother would mourn but she always kept us moving.

Growing up fast, we would soon go our separate ways and try to survive the streets on our own. Some of my siblings did this and I never sensed them again or saw them again. Most of the humans weren't so kind; they would hurt us or be cruel and we lost another one of my siblings. Some people are cruel, we learned that quickly. Never understood how they could be so cruel to us and how they themselves survived being the way they were.

I learned very fast that humans were not to be trusted but I also learned that some humans were kind, they petted us and gave us scraps.

As we kept wandering and resting when we could, trying to find food where we could, my mother left us in the blistering sun. She just fell, and I couldn't get her up again, I never sensed her again.

I cried in the noise that surrounded us, but no one ever stopped to help, even when I cried louder. I wish I could talk to anyone or stop them to help but they just kept walking not bothering to look back. The the way these humans just pass on by is so bad, especially for a lost pup. I would never be capable of doing what they did, perhaps this is why I'm me. I laid down beside Mother and nuzzled her one last time before getting up and moving like she had taught me. I said my goodbyes and looked at her one last time. It was now just me and some of my only siblings that remained; the rest had gone off; they had found their own fates.

I stopped one day, tired of moving, I could no longer go on and I was covered in bites and who knows what else I was no longer able to keep moving. My last sibling nuzzled me to say goodbye. I moved and heard my sibling crying as I closed my eyes; all the noise faded; I only hope my sibling would be okay, he was my pack after all.

I woke to some human noises that scared me. I closed my eyes once more.

When I next woke, I couldn't understand what was going on, but I felt stronger. I was surviving, I got moved around a lot. I had constant food. The humans I was with made me happy and gave me the rest I needed. I was happy.

Then when I was strong enough, I saw the giant pack of others, all kinds of others like me and they received lots of attention too. I had never seen so many of us in one place. The people constantly feeding us and being gentle and nice, not pushing us away. I felt safe and happy. I cried and people came to me to see if I needed anything. It was strange, they didn't ignore us like others always did. These humans were different.

There were lots of others like me here with different smells; older and younger were all treated the same, this place was so different. I started looking for my sibling to see if I could find him. This human looked at me and picked me up like she knew what I wanted now that I was able to move and felt so much stronger. She took me to a different area.

I found my sibling; he looked very happy to see me and we played so much that we were happy and healthy.

We were at this place a long time being cared for by a wonderful human who smiled and laughed at us being us and the rest of the people were the same. I felt loved.

I noticed slowly as some of my new friends began to leave these hard things that they couldn't get out of. I couldn't sense them again they never came back again. I never knew what happened to them. I hoped that they were happy and loved like this place I was in.

My sibling disappeared one day, like the others he was put in a place that he couldn't get out of. The human told me he was going somewhere better and that from what I understood would be happy.

I never saw him again, I felt sad and scared. One day another human came and gave me the warmest hug and so much love. I heard her say my name, "Yen, Yen," and something else I didn't understand then, and she said something to someone I didn't recognize, but I didn't know what it was. She looked sad, so I gave her a nuzzle and put my paw on her hand and she smiled happily.

I felt sad, I didn't know how to help her.

One of the people that was always there took me and gave me a "bath and trim" what they called it to me; it wasn't very pleasant; they grabbed my paw gently it felt unpleasant, I saw one on my favorite toys in a hard-shell I'd seen others go in. I went to retrieve my toy, and I was trapped; I couldn't get out! I was scared and cried out but then I was put with others in similar hard things, they were also crying out as well. I didn't know what to do.

This is the end, I thought they put me in a very dark place, and I heard a very loud noise that scared me, but I couldn't run. It was such a long time until the noise stopped, I never slept the whole time. Something I had learned from my days travelling the streets was, always be alert.

Finally, I saw the brightness of this new place, where there were so many different smells and new noises I'd never heard before. I was carried away by some people smiling and looking very happy. I felt their love through my hard box.

When I finally stopped moving, I was at this new place, smaller than before, with this new human, who seemed very happy to have me in there. I stayed in my box as I didn't know what to do. They always talked about me and looked at me a lot; they gave me food and took me around my new surroundings, they always made sure to touch me lots and they really seemed to be happy I was there.

They allowed me to come to them; they weren't forceful, and they didn't push me. They gave me space but still lots of love and even lots of nuzzles, which I didn't know what to do.

These humans brought me to their home, were patient with me and showed me not to be afraid, and that they love me completely and that I am family. I feel completely safe and happy.

I look back at my old life, which I can hardly remember. I wish people could see that we aren't bad; we do what we can to survive as everyone does, and once we find our homes and our humans, we depend on them to help us grow, learn, and we love them unconditionally they are as much a part of us as we are of them.

Don't look away from us when you are in the streets or anywhere you are. If we need help, help by finding our forever home and helping us Find Our Way Home.

The End

www.ingramcontent.com/pod-product-compliance
Lightning Source LLC
Chambersburg PA
CBHW051835170626
46807CB00003B/1192